DISCOVER GRAPHICS

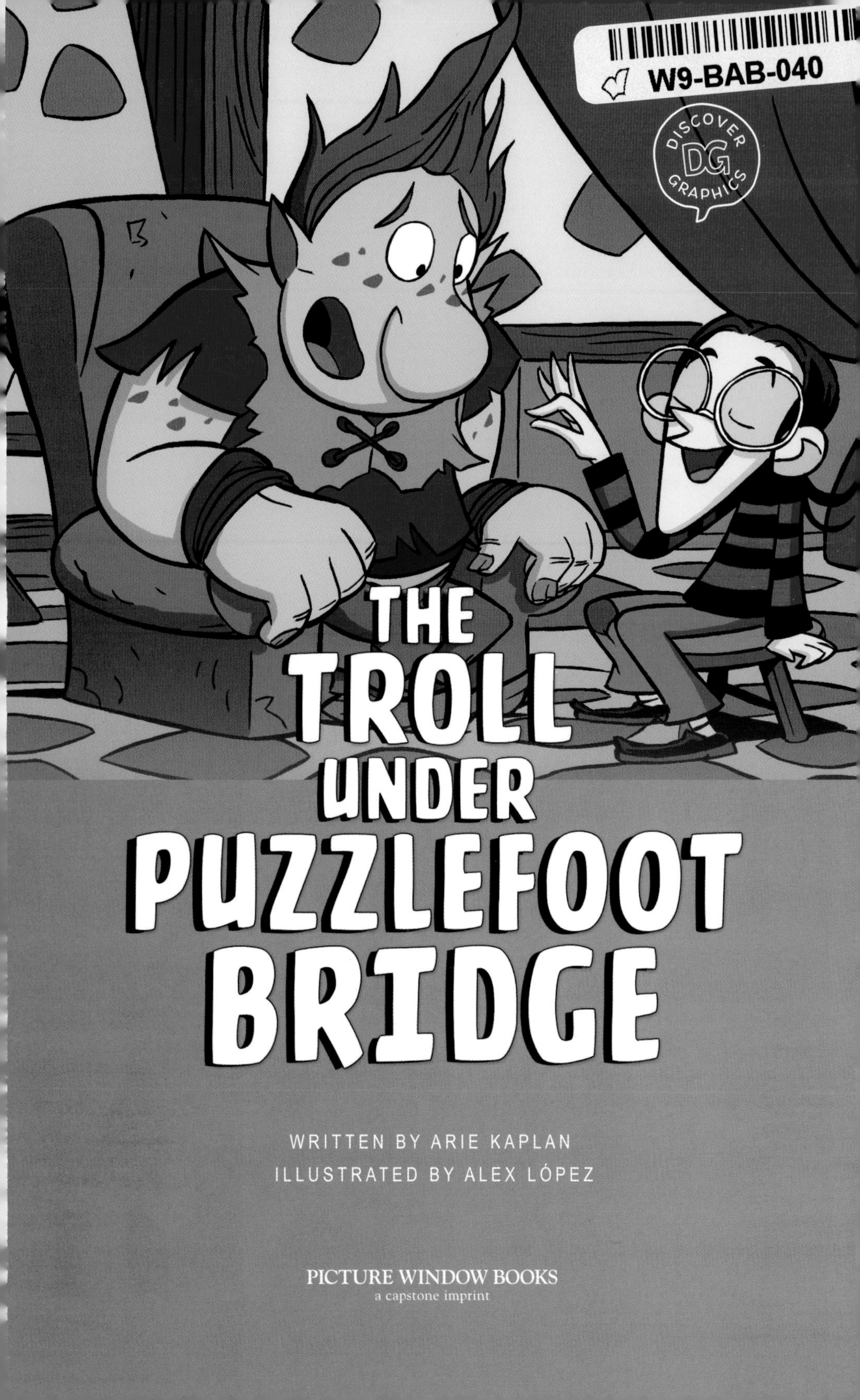

THE TROLL UNDER PUZZLEFOOT BRIDGE

WRITTEN BY ARIE KAPLAN
ILLUSTRATED BY ALEX LÓPEZ

PICTURE WINDOW BOOKS
a capstone imprint

Discover Graphics is published by Picture Window Books,
an imprint of Capstone.
1710 Roe Crest Drive
North Mankato, Minnesota 56003
www.capstonepub.com

Library of Congress Cataloging-in-Publication Data
Names: Kaplan, Arie, author. | Lopez, Alex, 1971– illustrator.
Title: The troll under Puzzlefoot Bridge / by Arie Kaplan ;
   illustrated by Alex Lopez.
Description: North Mankato, Minnesota : Picture Window Books,
   a Capstone imprint, [2021] | Series: Discover graphics. Mythical
   creatures | Audience: Ages 5–7. | Audience: Grades K–1.
Identifiers: LCCN 2020031424 (print) | LCCN 2020031425 (ebook) |
   ISBN 9781515882053 (hardcover) | ISBN 9781515883104
   (paperback) | ISBN 9781515892458 (eBook PDF) | ISBN 9781515892700
   (kindle edition)
Subjects: LCSH: Graphic novels. | CYAC: Graphic novels. | Trolls—
   Fiction. | Body swapping—Fiction. | Magic—Fiction. | Friendship—Fiction.
Classification: LCC PZ7.7.K37 Ts 2021 (print) | LCC PZ7.7.K37
   (ebook) | DDC 741.5/973—dc23
LC record available at https://lccn.loc.gov/2020031424
LC ebook record available at https://lccn.loc.gov/2020031425

Summary: When Noah Gruelle explores under Puzzlefoot Bridge, he's
surprised to find a troll living there! Then a mysterious spell causes them
to switch places, and they must learn how to live in each other's skins.

Editorial Credits:
Editor: Mari Bolte; Designer: Kay Fraser; Media Researcher:
Tracy Cummins; Production Specialist: Katy LaVigne

*Dedicated to my wife, Nadine Graham, who found me when I was but a troll living under
a bridge and taught me to live amongst human beings. I am forever grateful. —AK*

WORDS TO KNOW

curse—an evil spell meant to harm someone

founder—someone who sets up or starts something

lyric—the words of a song

Printed and bound in the USA. PO 3837

CAST OF CHARACTERS

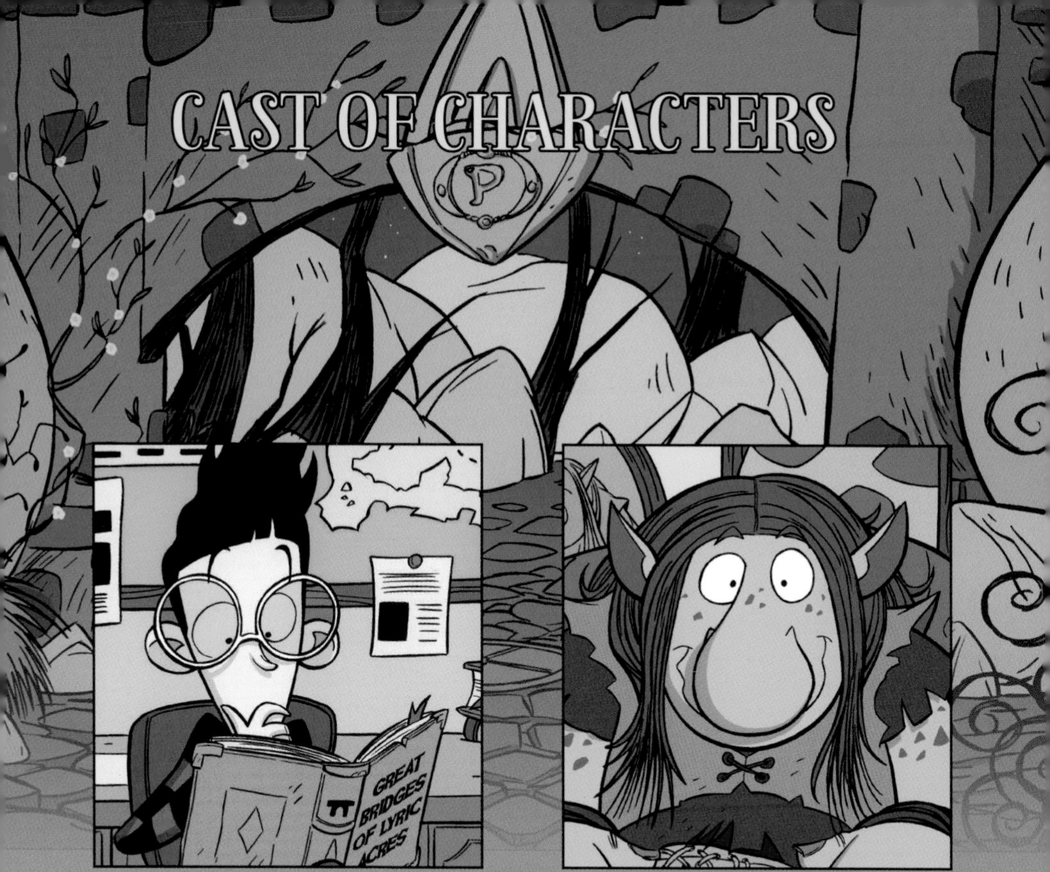
GREAT BRIDGES OF LYRIC ACRES

Noah is a human boy. His interest in old bridges gets him into trouble.

Torvald is a troll. He lives alone under Puzzlefoot Bridge.

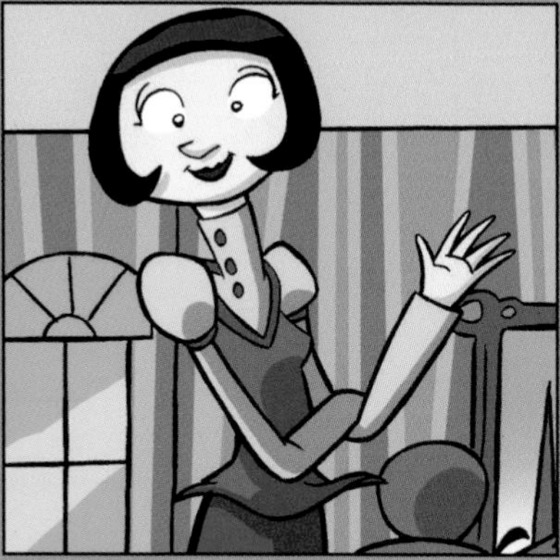

Prunella is Noah's mom.

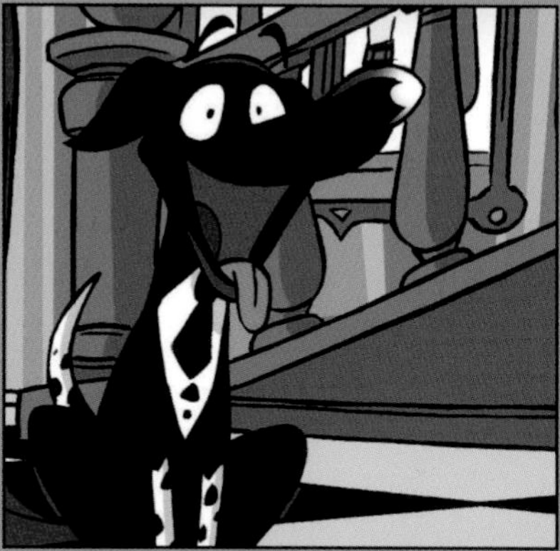

Tuxedo is Noah's dog.

HOW TO READ A GRAPHIC NOVEL

Graphic novels are easy to read. Boxes called panels show you how to follow the story. Look at the panels from left to right and top to bottom.

Read the word boxes and word balloons from left to right as well. Don't forget the sound and action words in the pictures.

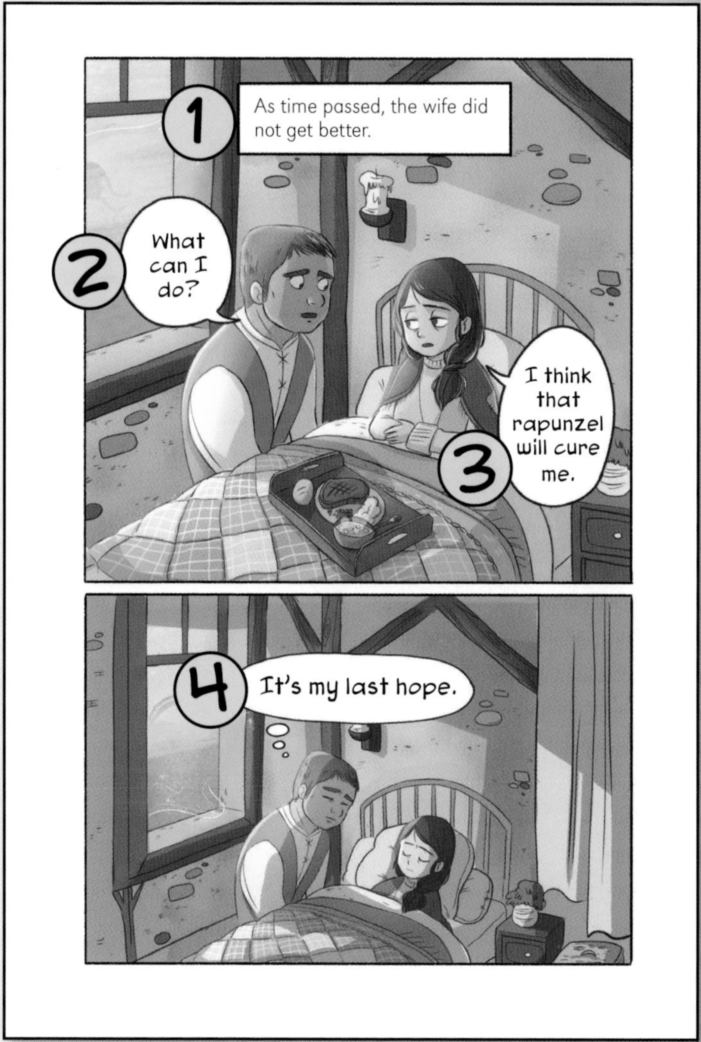
1
As time passed, the wife did not get better.
2
What can I do?
I think that rapunzel will cure me.
3
4
It's my last hope.

The pictures and the words work together to tell the whole story.

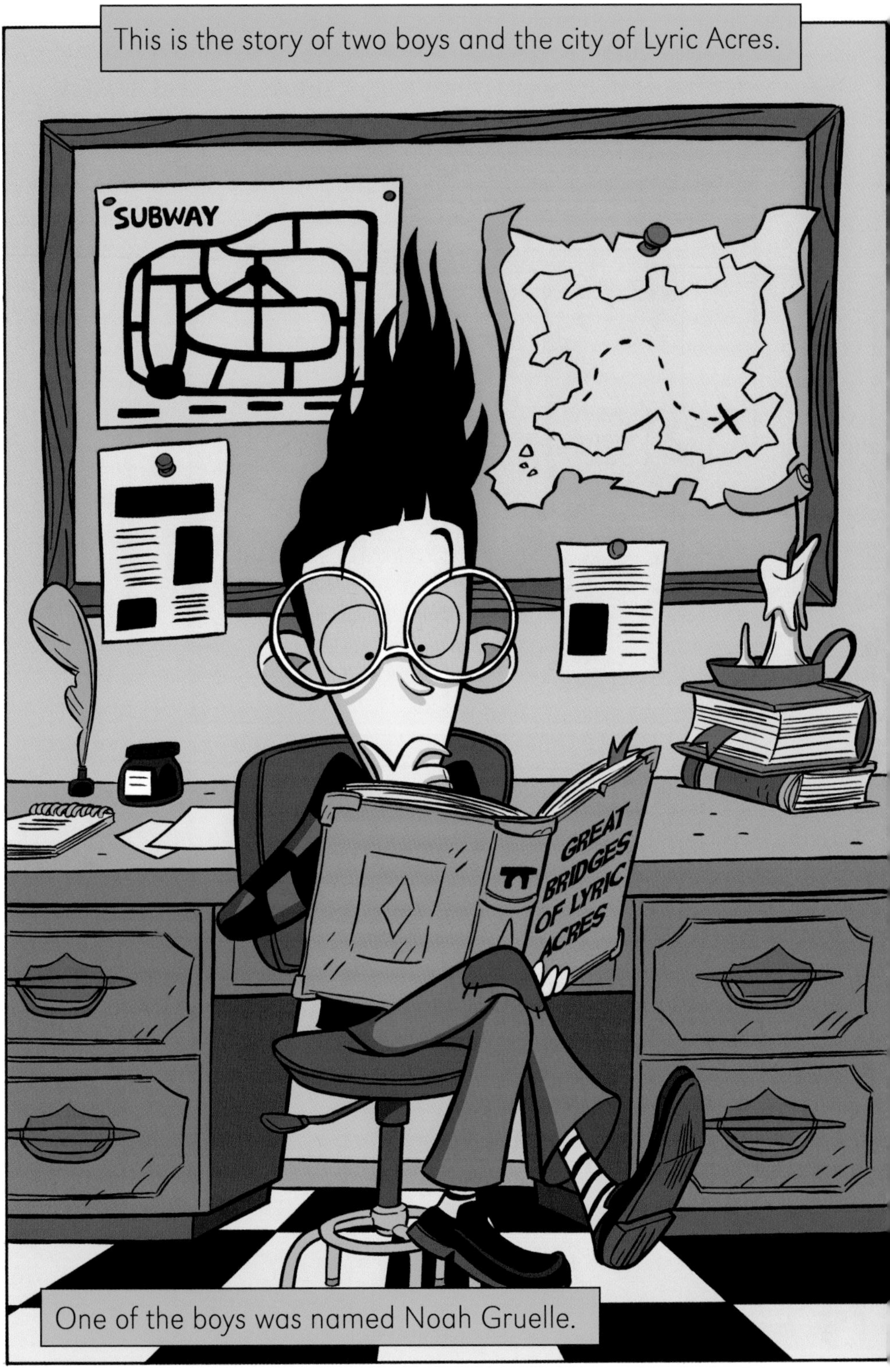

This is the story of two boys and the city of Lyric Acres.
SUBWAY
GREAT BRIDGES OF LYRIC ACRES
One of the boys was named Noah Gruelle.

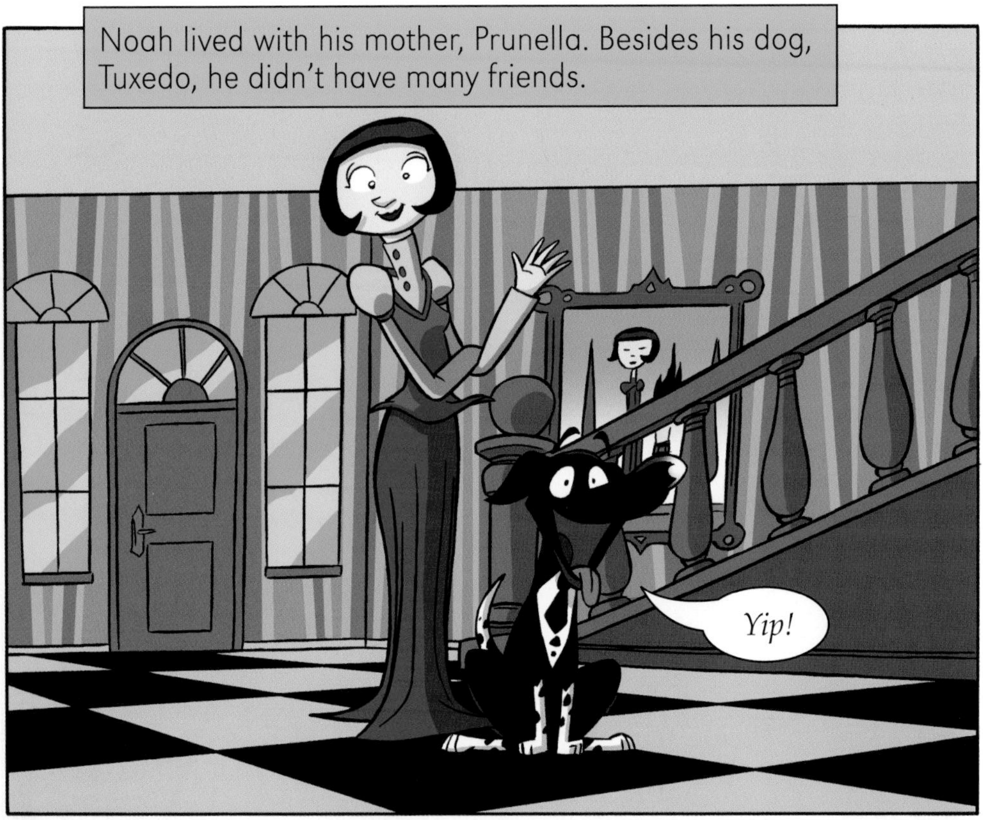
Noah lived with his mother, Prunella. Besides his dog, Tuxedo, he didn't have many friends.
Yip!

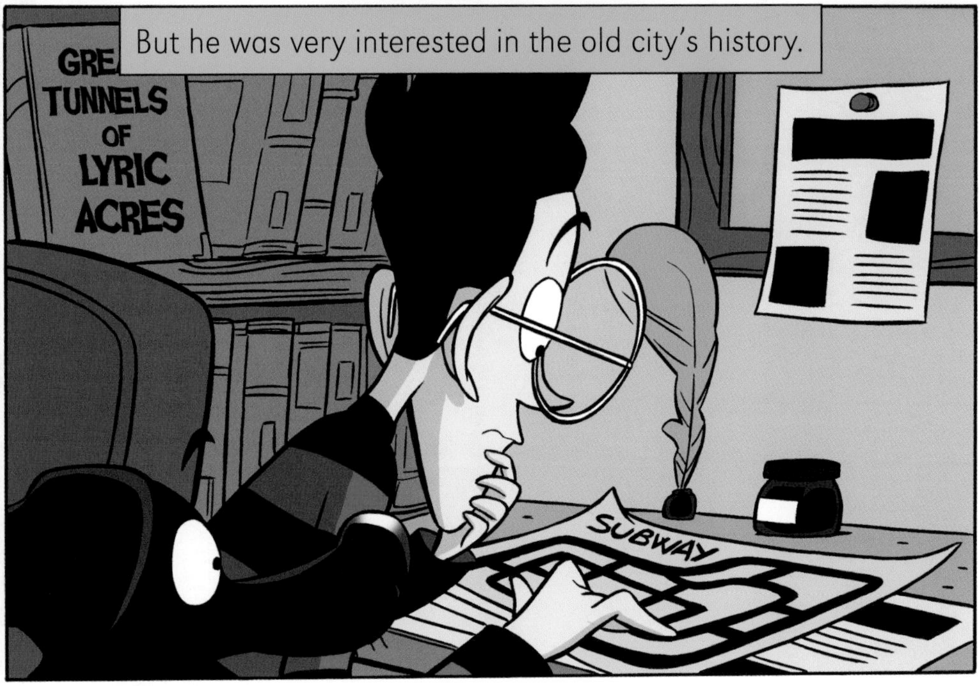
But he was very interested in the old city's history.
TUNNELS OF LYRIC ACRES
SUBWAY

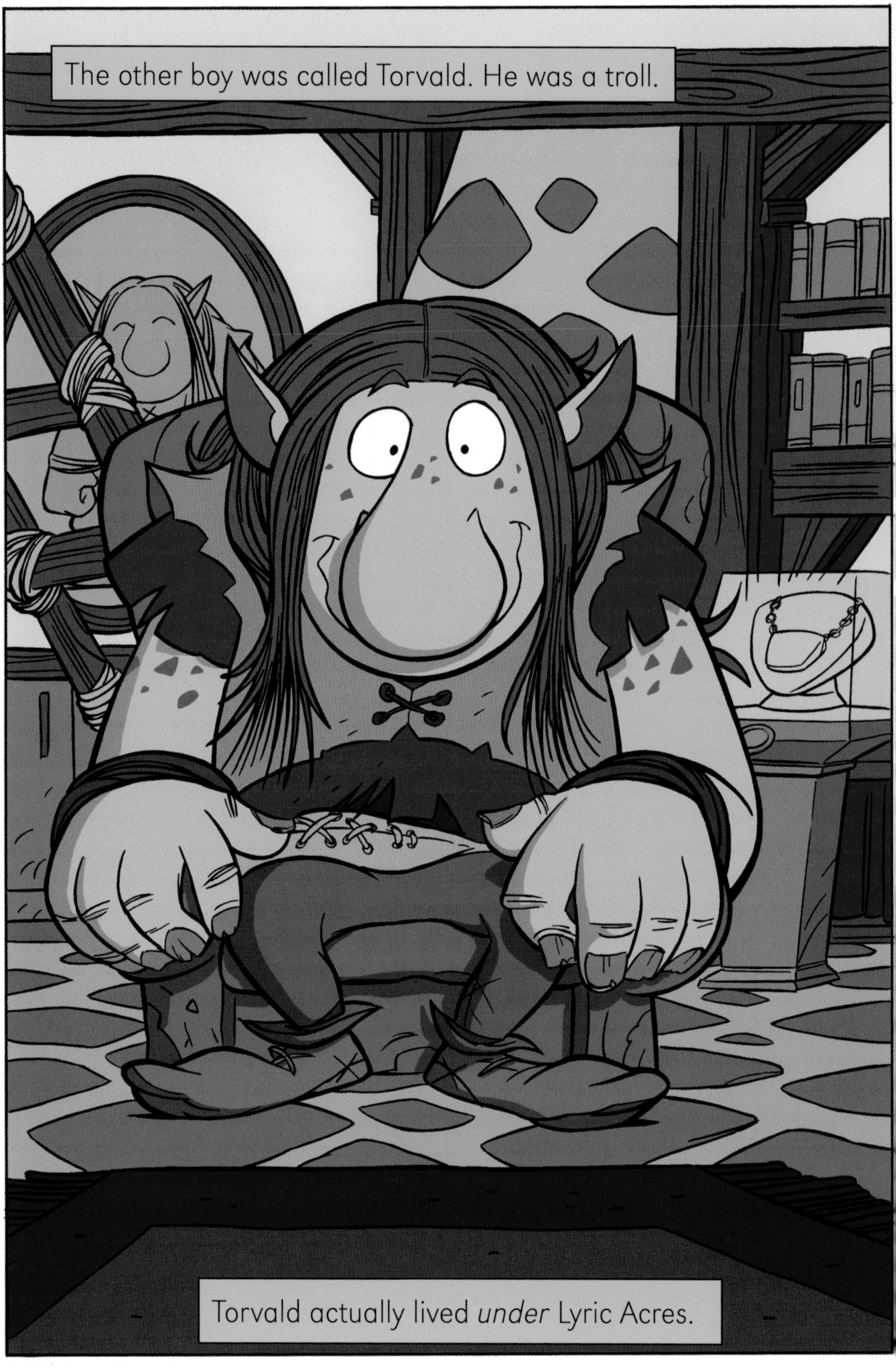
The other boy was called Torvald. He was a troll.
Torvald actually lived *under* Lyric Acres.

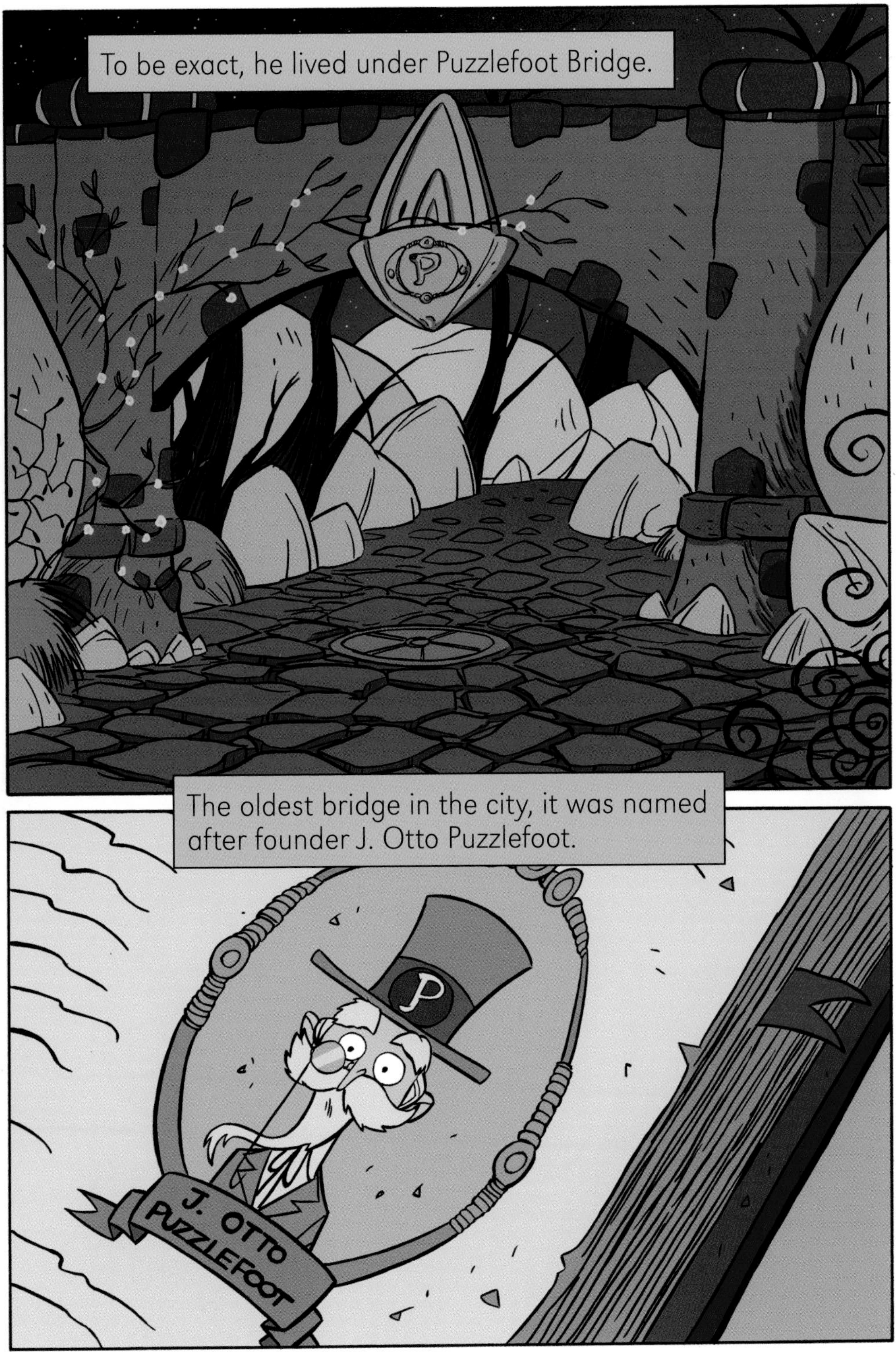
To be exact, he lived under Puzzlefoot Bridge.
The oldest bridge in the city, it was named after founder J. Otto Puzzlefoot.
J. OTTO PUZZLEFOOT

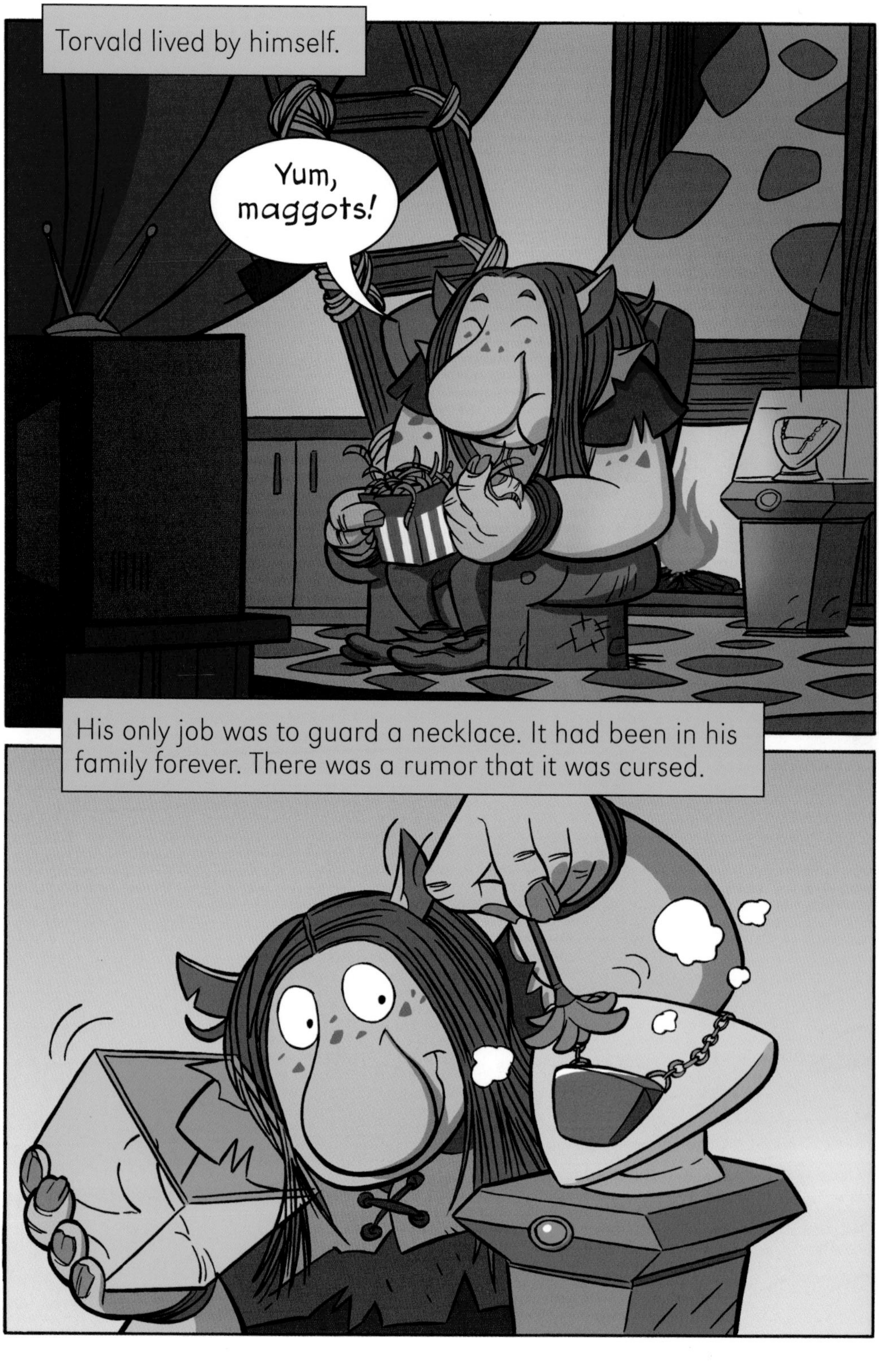
Torvald lived by himself.
Yum, maggots!
His only job was to guard a necklace. It had been in his family forever. There was a rumor that it was cursed.

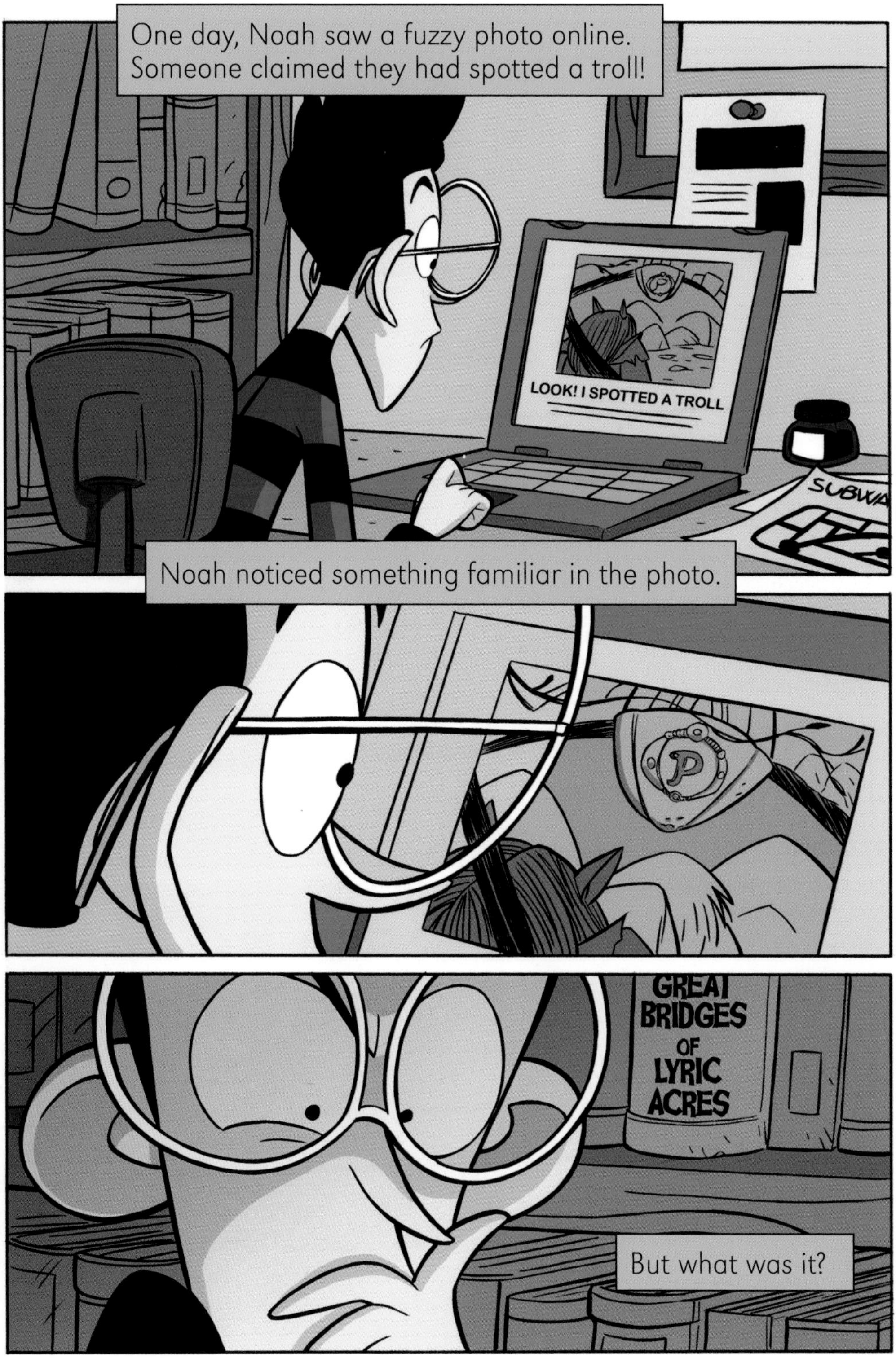

One day, Noah saw a fuzzy photo online.
Someone claimed they had spotted a troll!
LOOK! I SPOTTED A TROLL
Noah noticed something familiar in the photo.
GREAT BRIDGES OF LYRIC ACRES
But what was it?

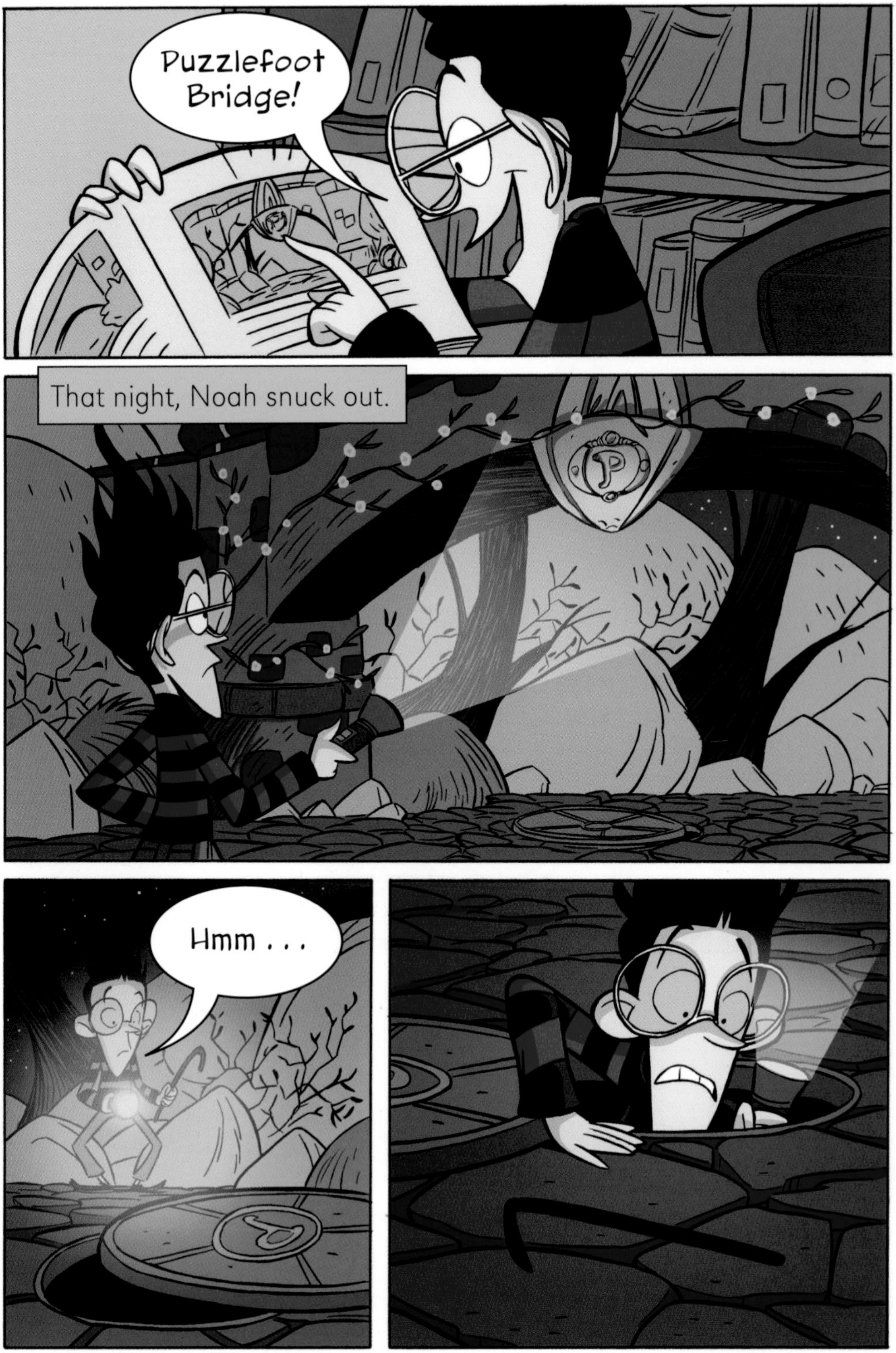

Puzzlefoot Bridge!
That night, Noah snuck out.
Hmm . . .

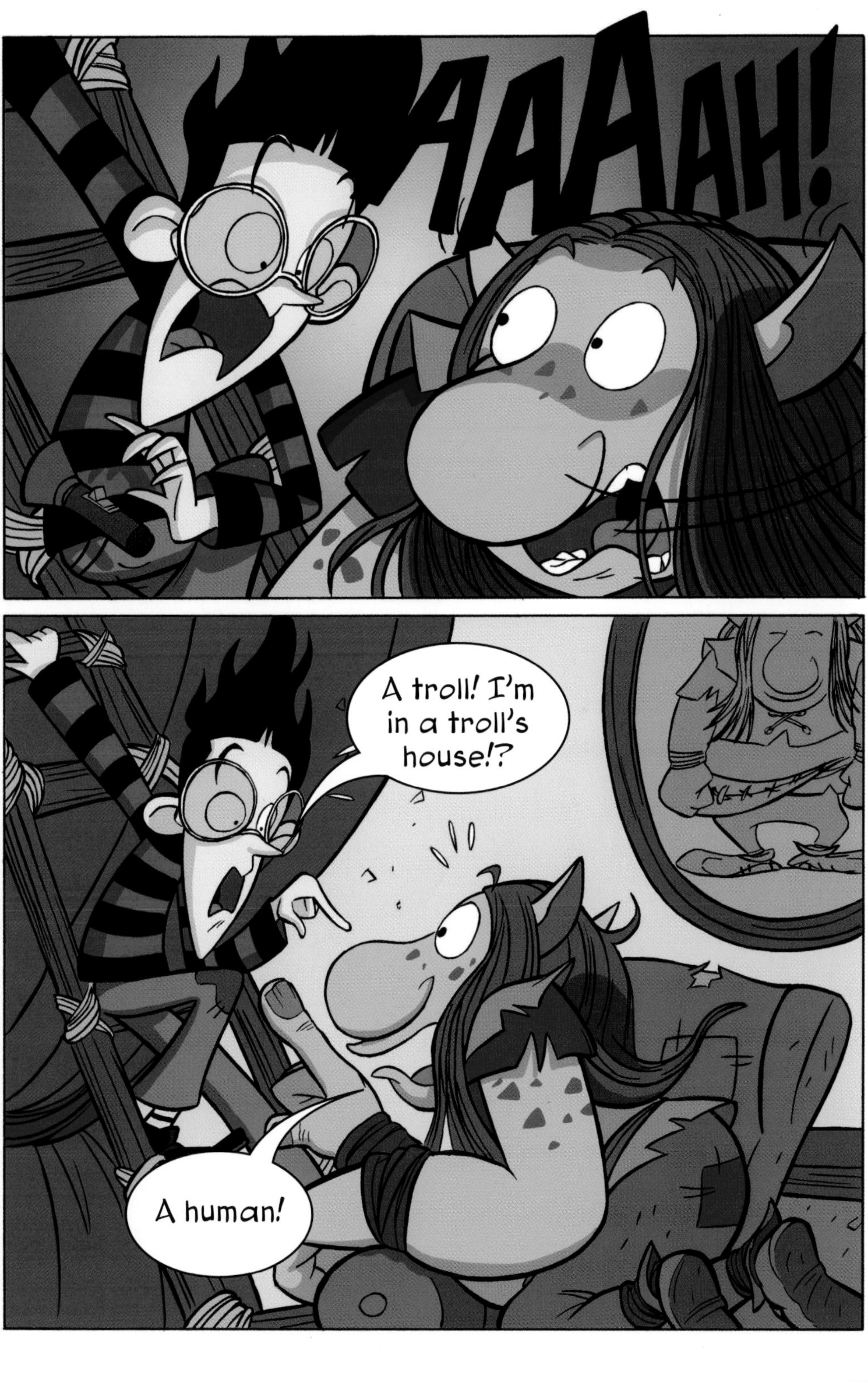
AAAAAH!
A troll! I'm in a troll's house!?
A human!

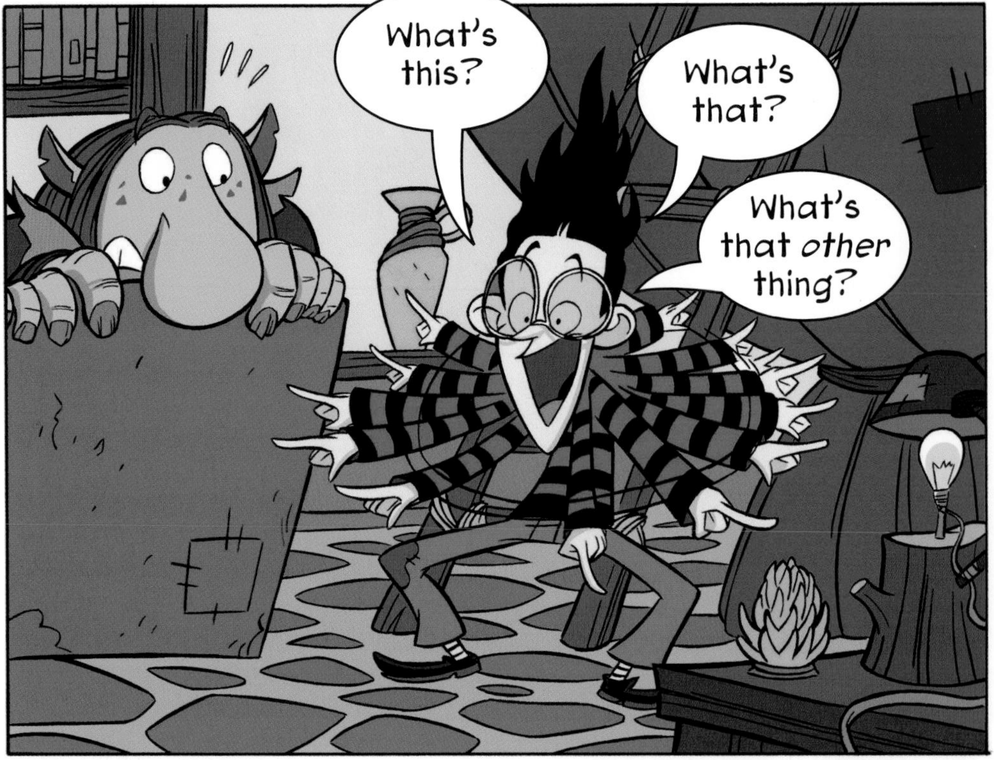
What's this?
What's that?
What's that *other* thing?

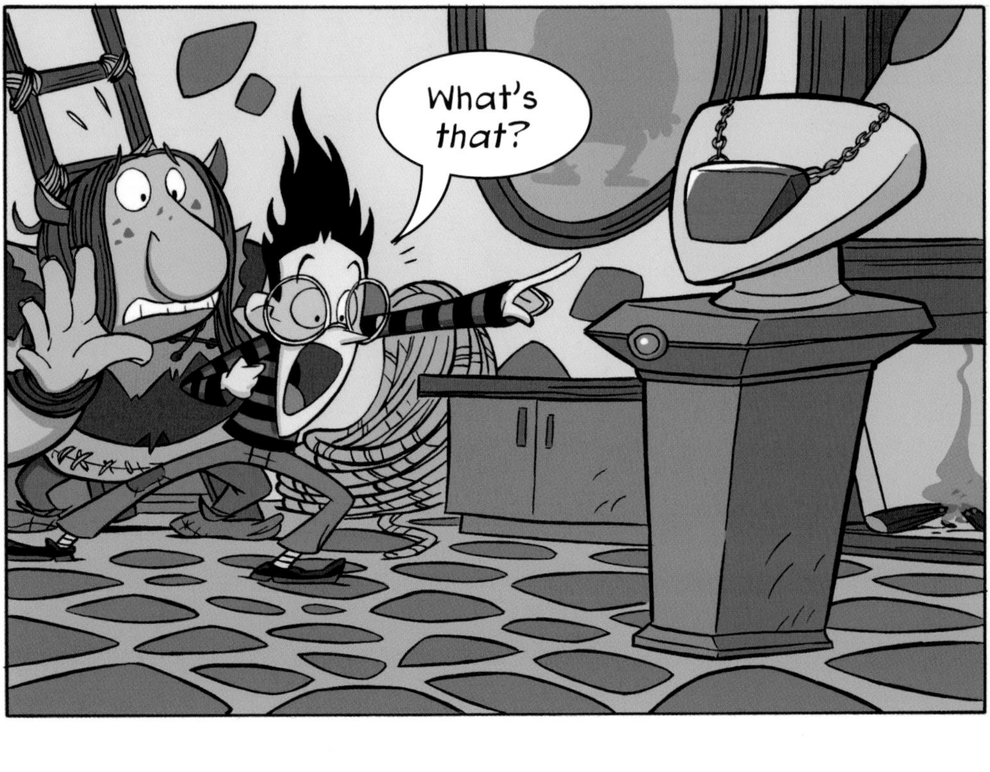
What's *that*?

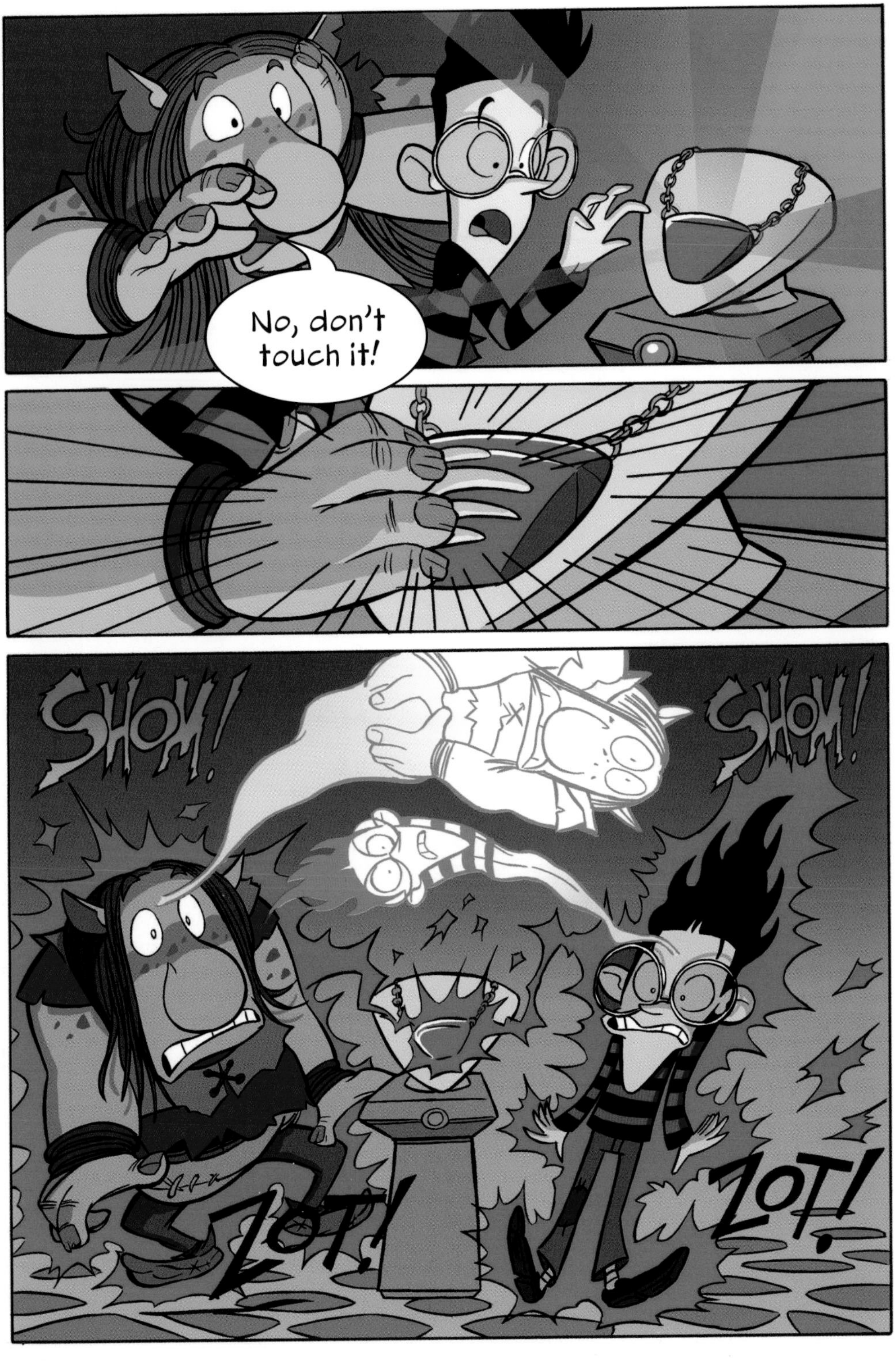

No, don't touch it!
SHOM!
SHOM!
ZOT!
ZOT!

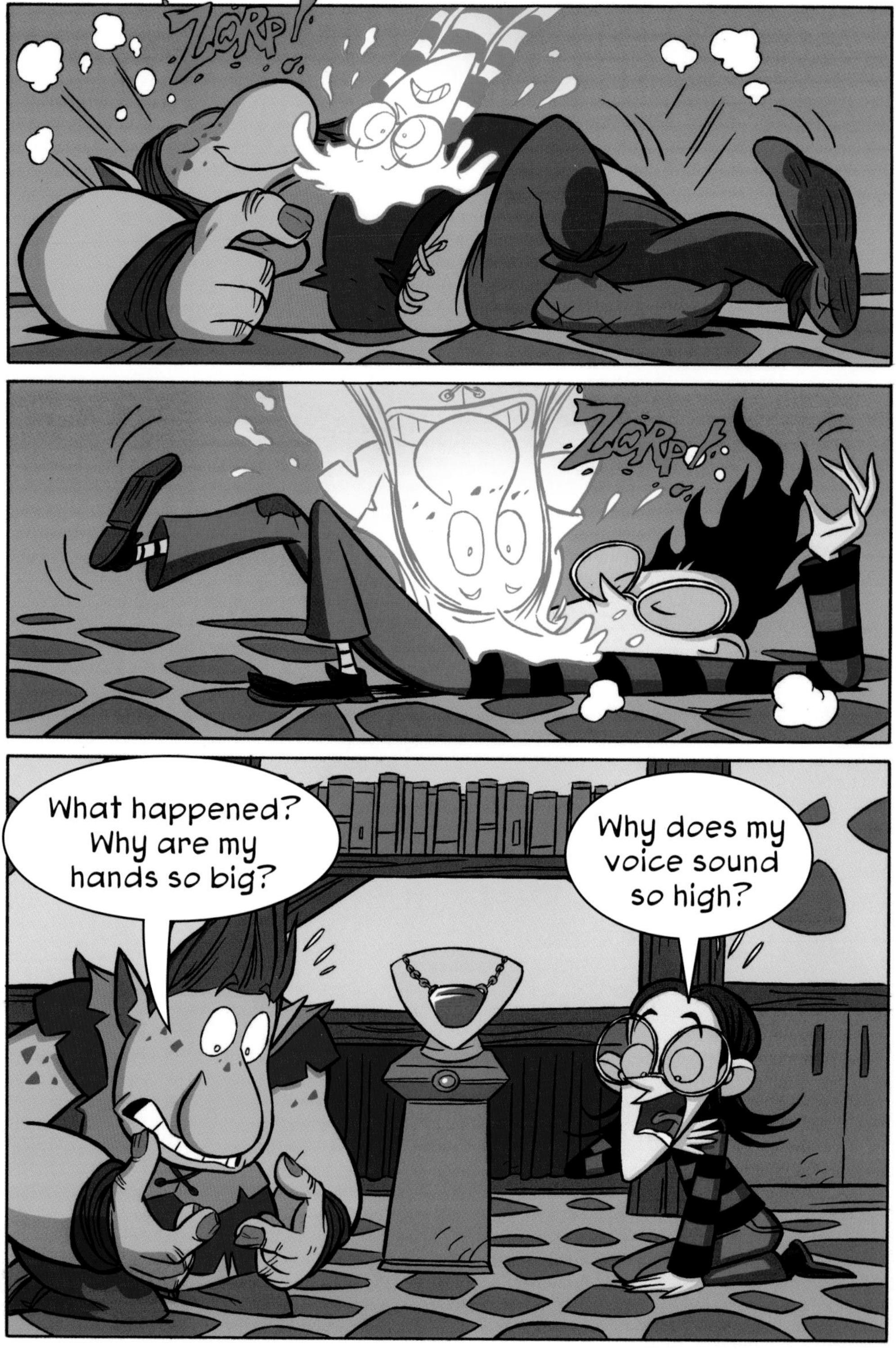
ZORP!
ZORP!
What happened? Why are my hands so big?
Why does my voice sound so high?

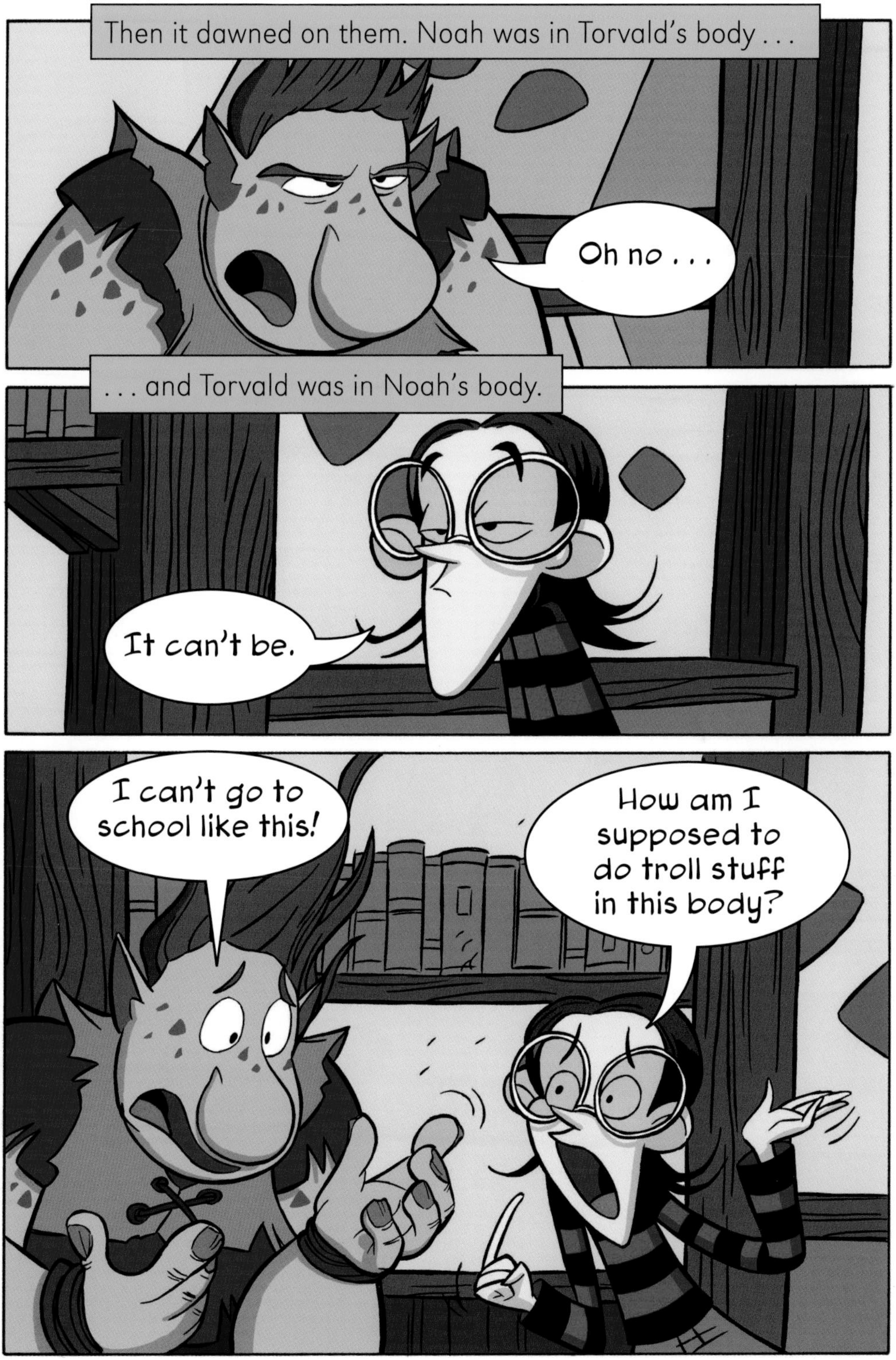
Then it dawned on them. Noah was in Torvald's body . . .
Oh no . . .
. . . and Torvald was in Noah's body.
It can't be.
I can't go to school like this!
How am I supposed to do troll stuff in this body?

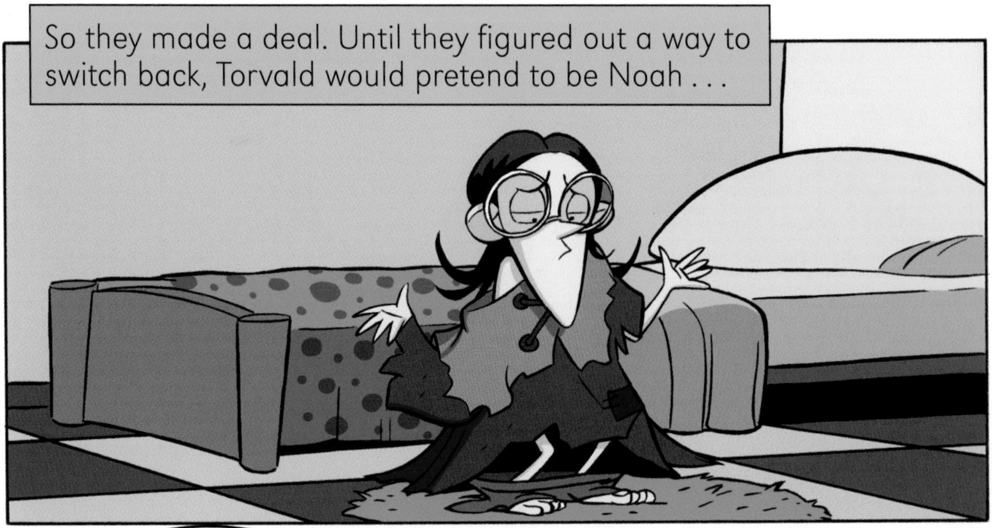
So they made a deal. Until they figured out a way to switch back, Torvald would pretend to be Noah . . .

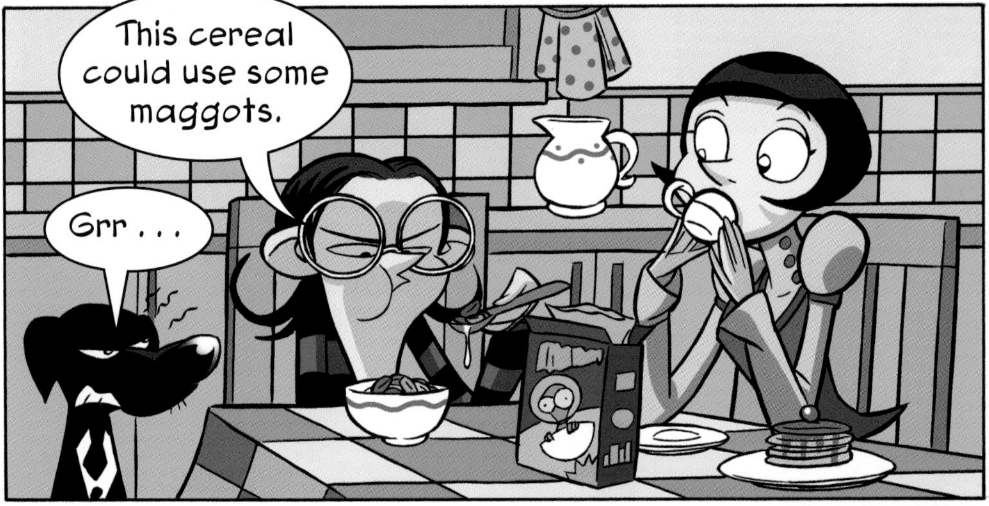
This cereal could use some maggots.
Grr . . .

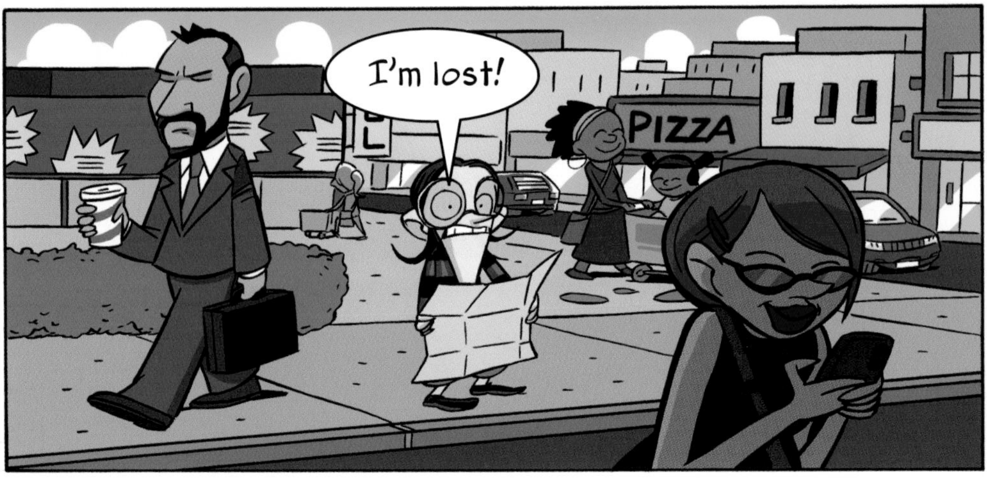
I'm lost!
PIZZA

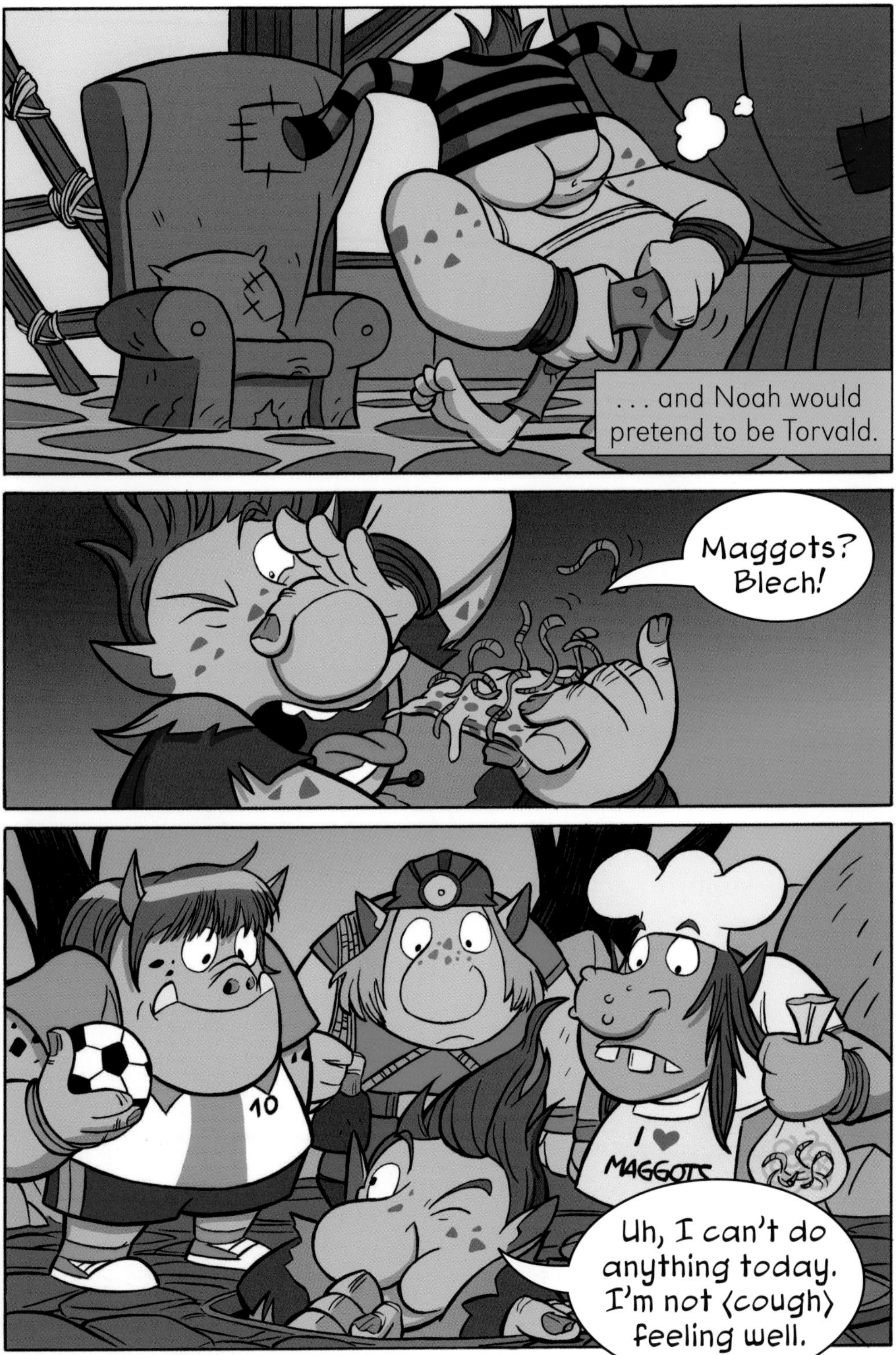
. . . and Noah would pretend to be Torvald.
Maggots? Blech!
Uh, I can't do anything today. I'm not (cough) feeling well.

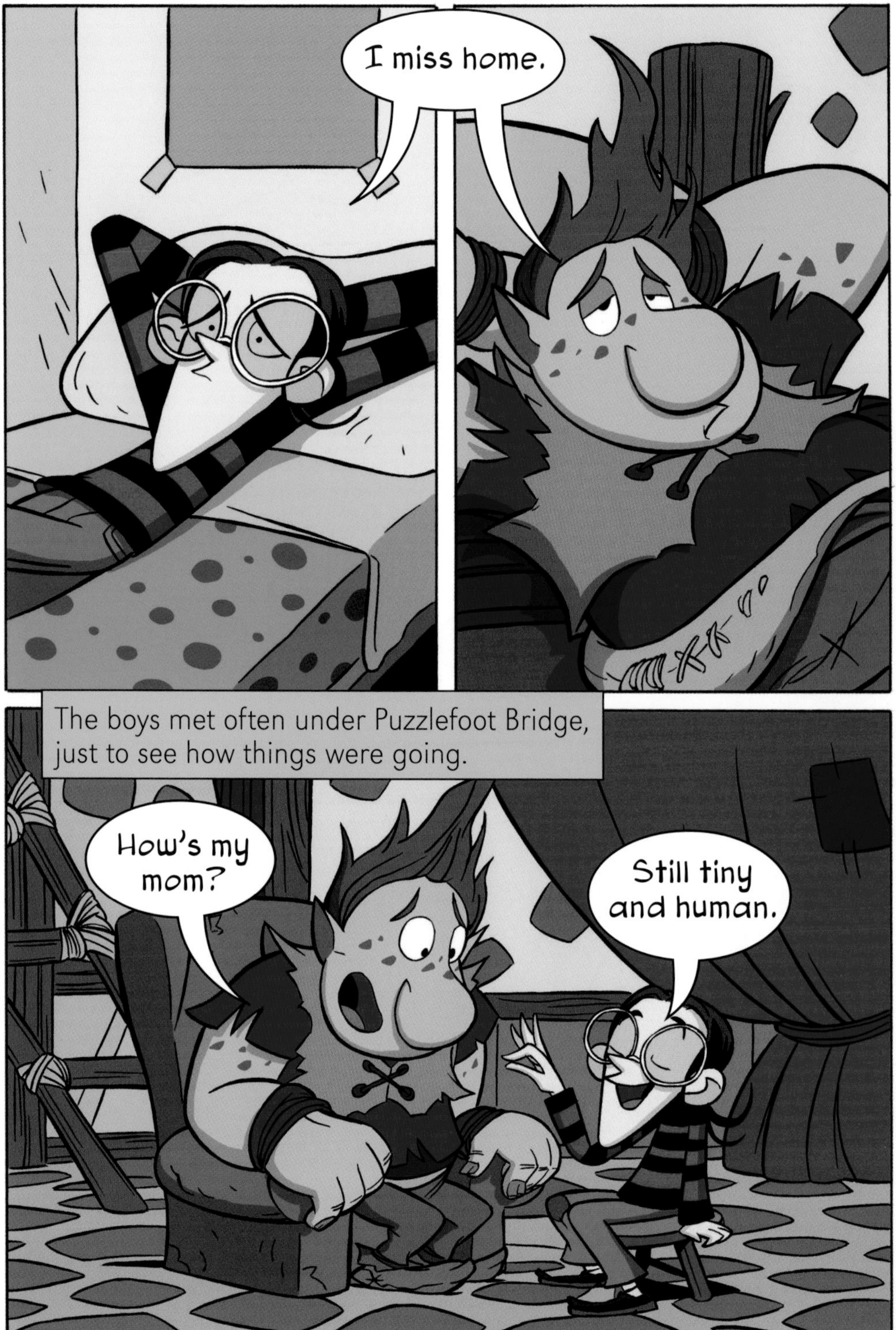
I miss home.
The boys met often under Puzzlefoot Bridge, just to see how things were going.
How's my mom?
Still tiny and human.

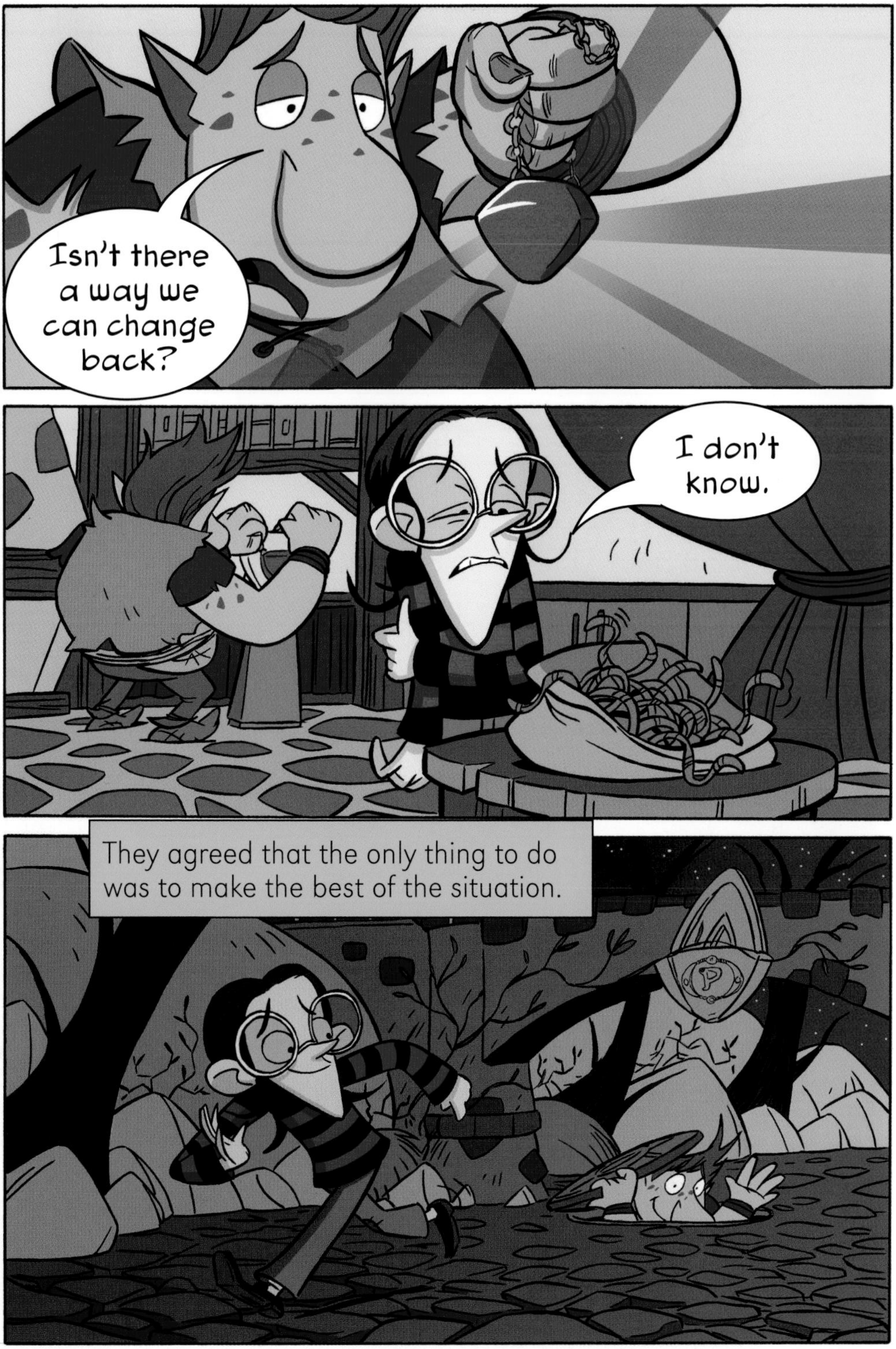
Isn't there a way we can change back?
I don't know.
They agreed that the only thing to do was to make the best of the situation.

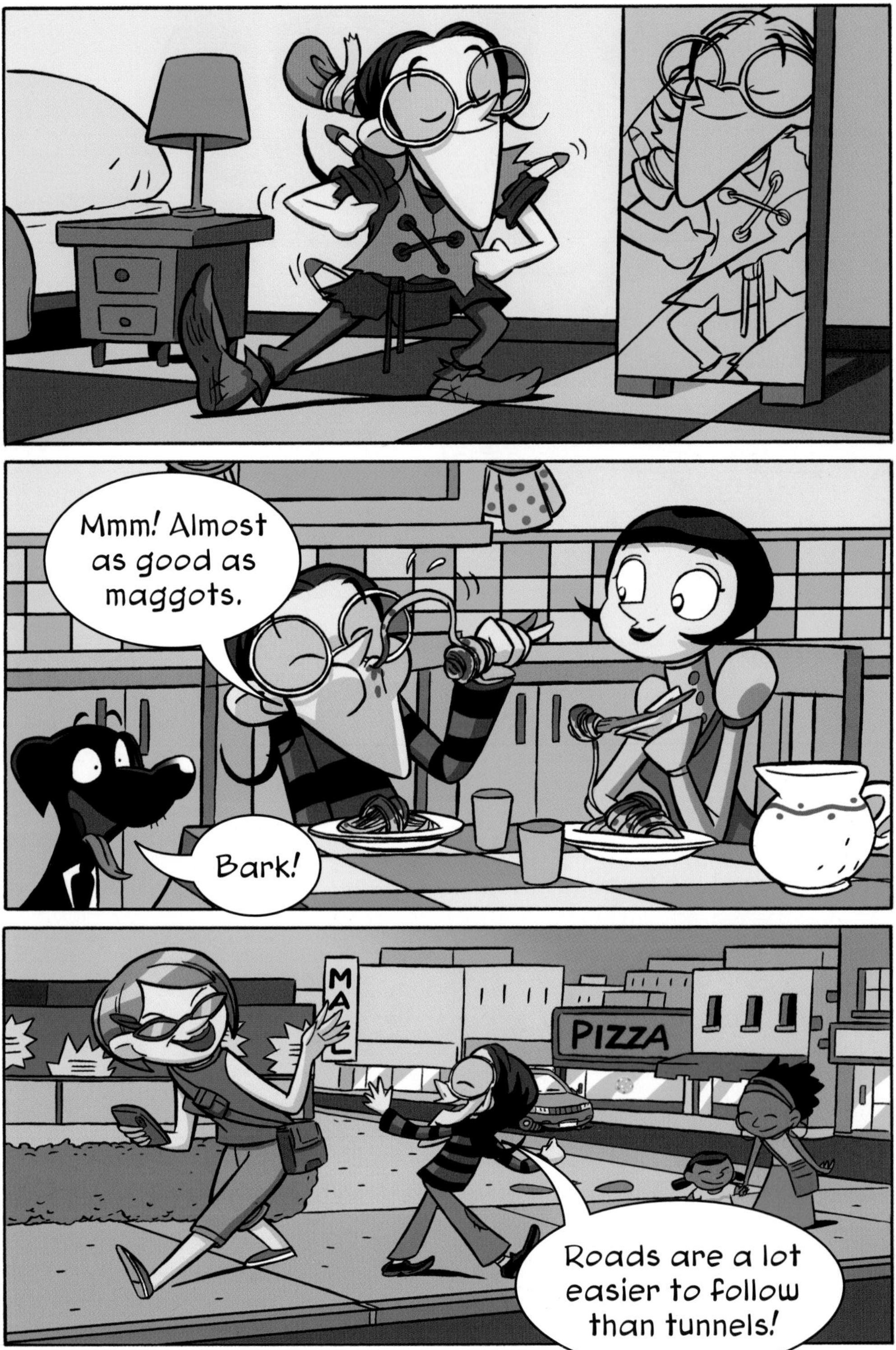
Mmm! Almost as good as maggots.
Bark!
PIZZA
Roads are a lot easier to follow than tunnels!

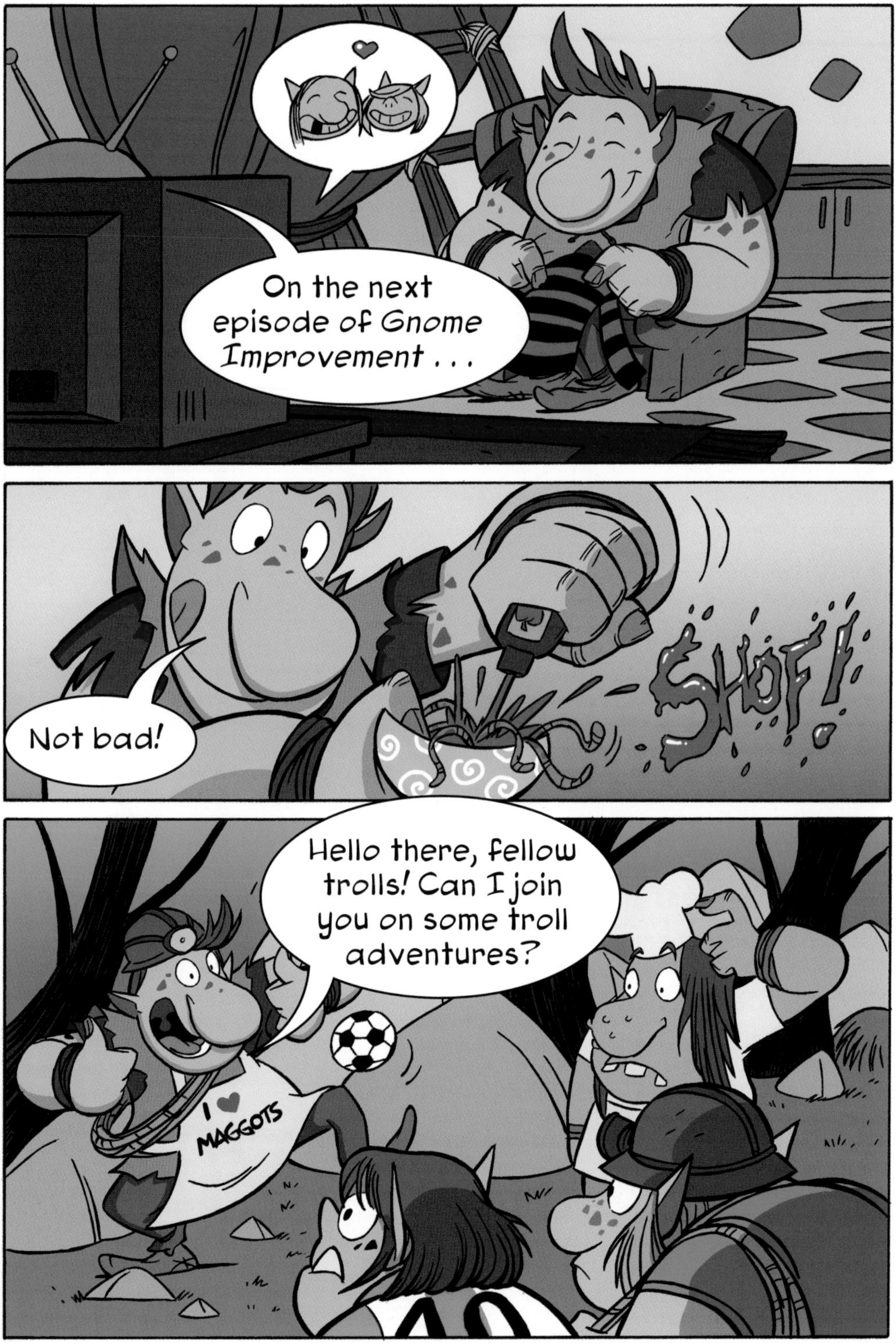
On the next episode of Gnome Improvement . . .
Not bad!
SHOF!
Hello there, fellow trolls! Can I join you on some troll adventures?
I ♥ MAGGOTS

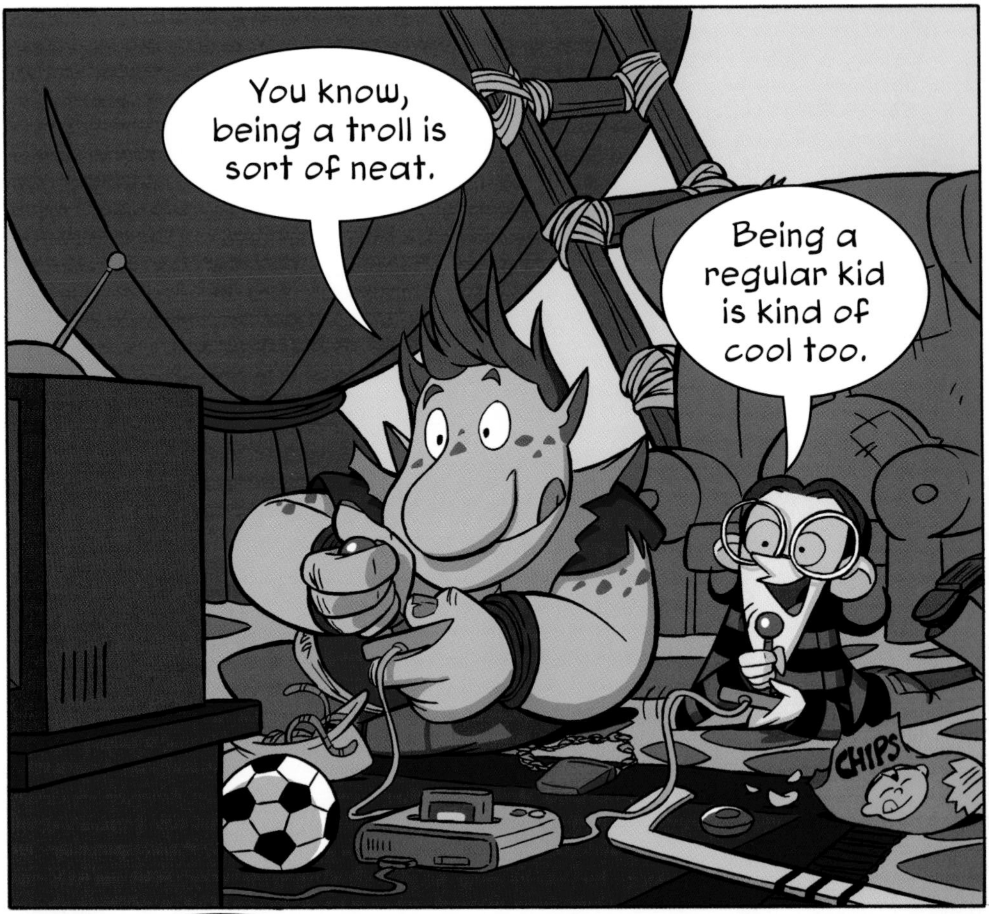
You know, being a troll is sort of neat.
Being a regular kid is kind of cool too.
CHIPS

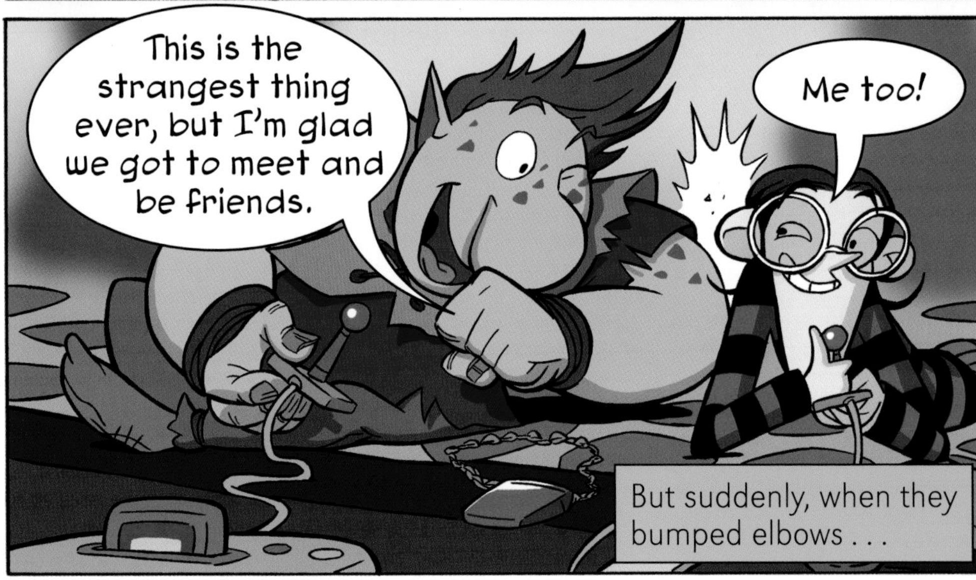
This is the strangest thing ever, but I'm glad we got to meet and be friends.
Me too!
But suddenly, when they bumped elbows . . .

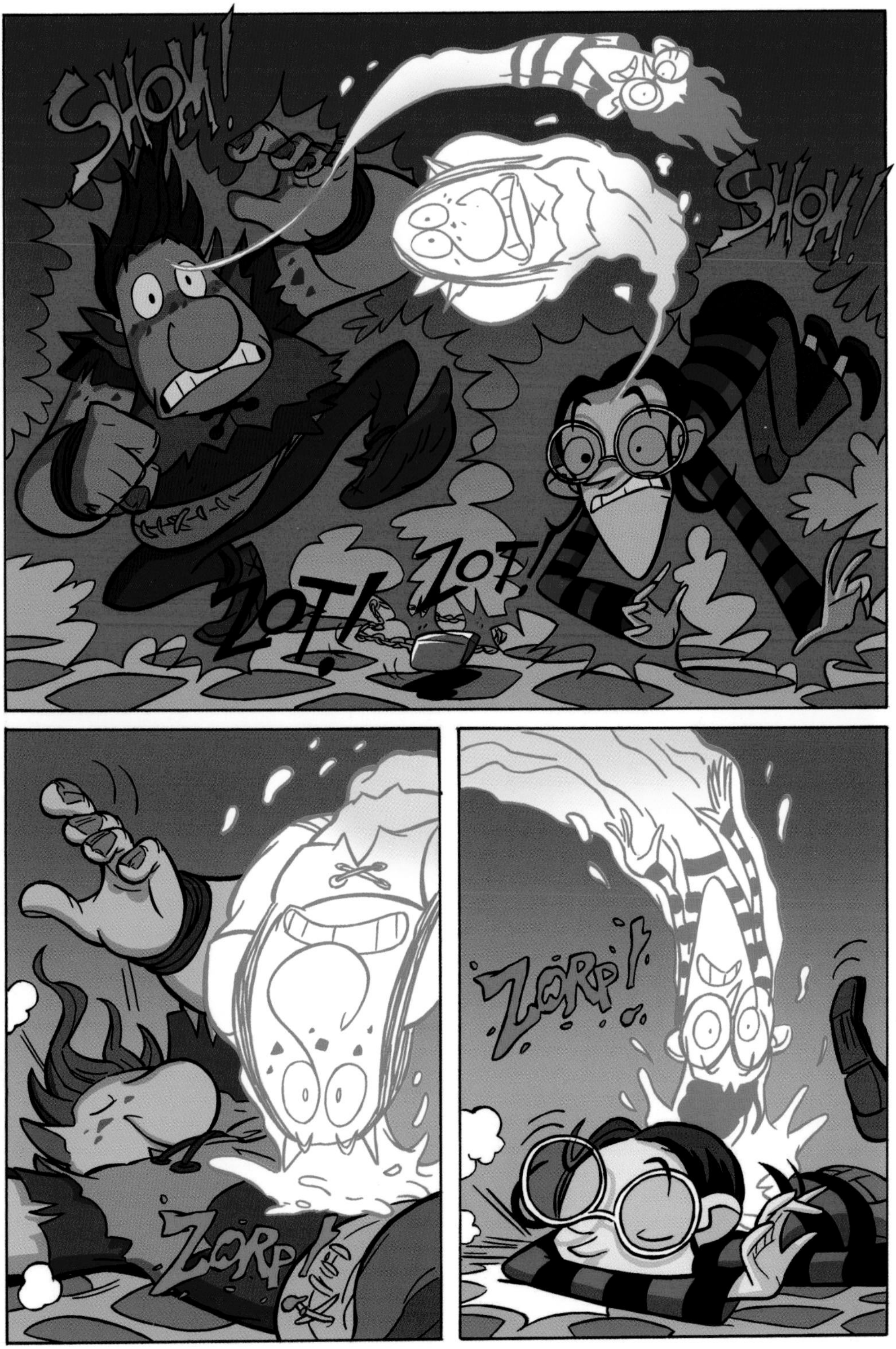
SHOM!
SHOM!
ZOT!
ZOT!
ZORP!
ZORP!

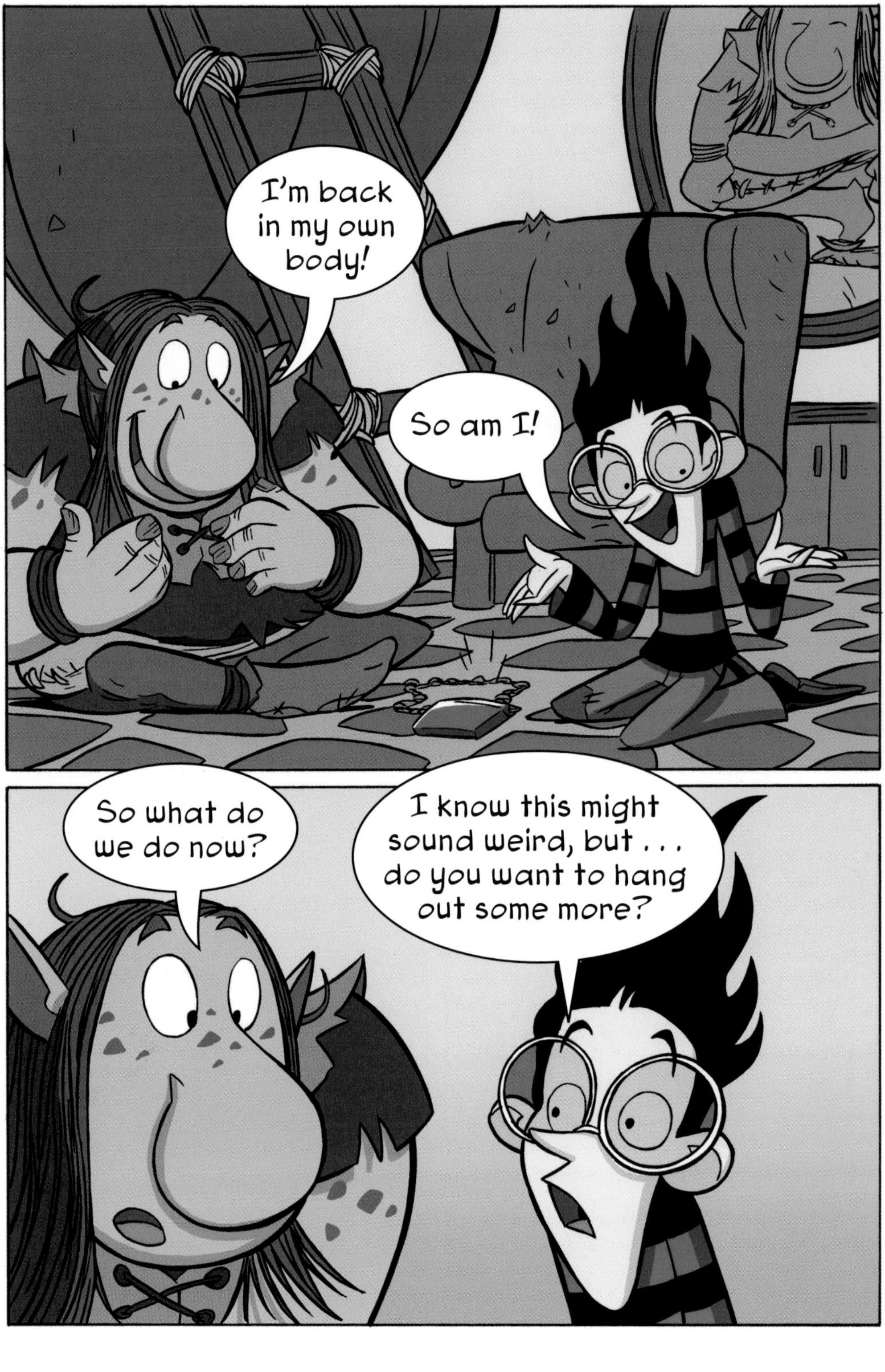
I'm back in my own body!
So am I!
So what do we do now?
I know this might sound weird, but . . . do you want to hang out some more?

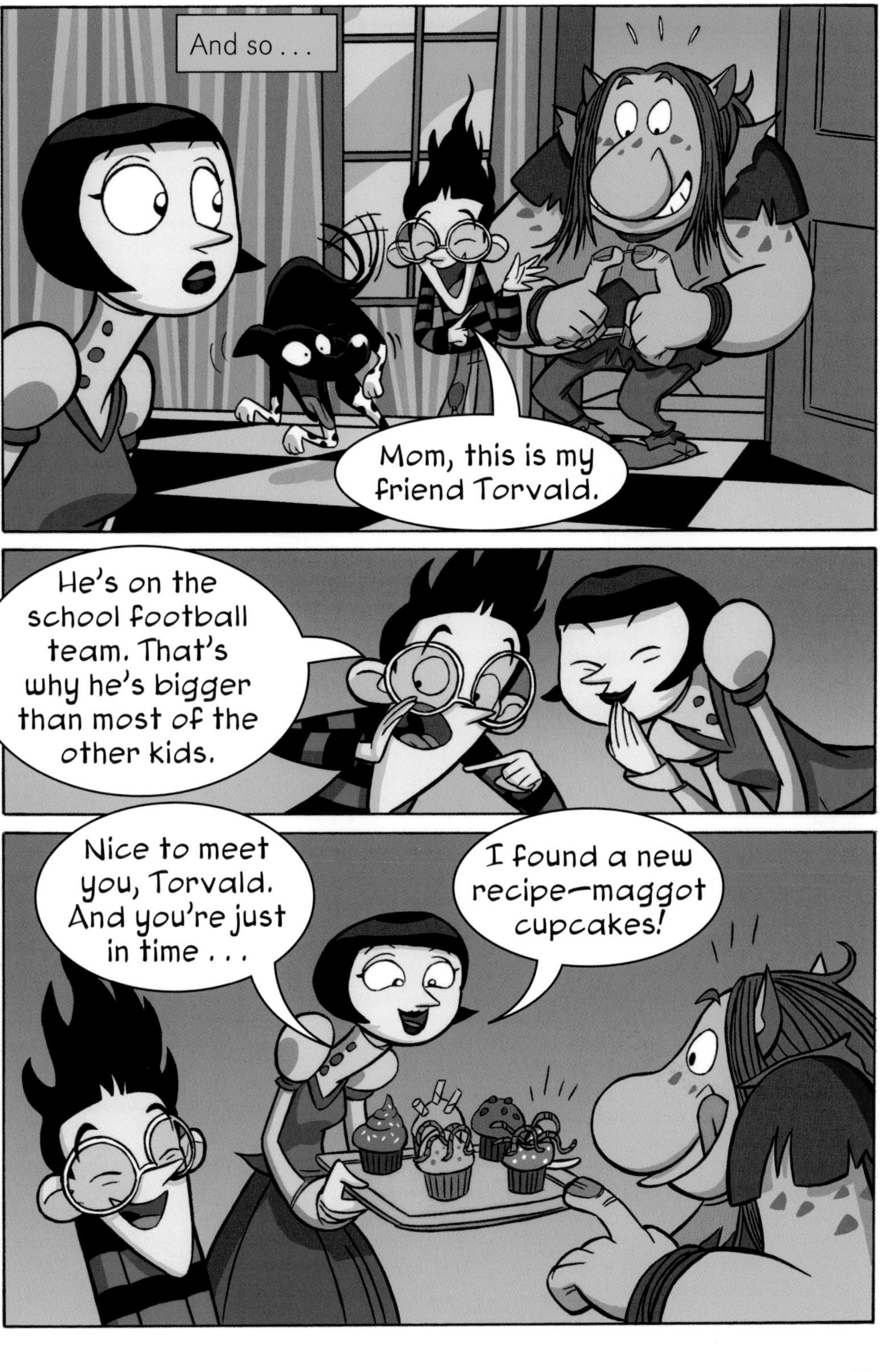
And so . . .
Mom, this is my friend Torvald.
He's on the school football team. That's why he's bigger than most of the other kids.
Nice to meet you, Torvald. And you're just in time . . .
I found a new recipe—maggot cupcakes!

WRITING PROMPTS

1. What is Torvald's favorite food? Invent a recipe using that ingredient.

2. Noah likes learning about his city. Write a paragraph describing your favorite part of the city where you live.

3. Puzzlefoot Bridge is an old, historic bridge. Are there any historic landmarks where you live? Write a paragraph about one you like.

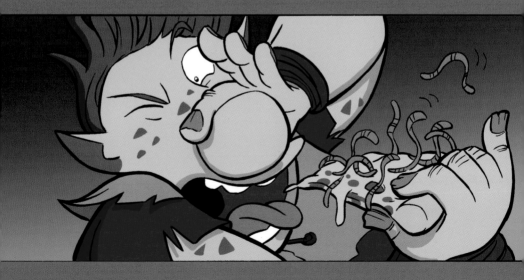

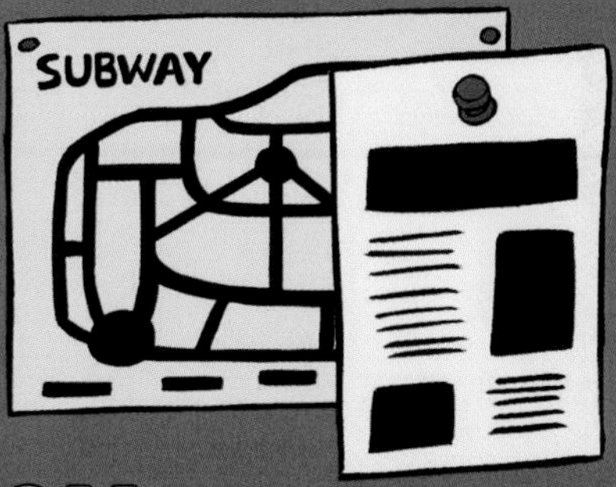
SUBWAY

DISCUSSION QUESTIONS

1. When Noah and Torvald touch the amulet at the same time, what happens to them?
2. Re-read page 18. Why does Tuxedo growl when Torvald is in Noah's body?
3. How can you tell when the boys have switched bodies?

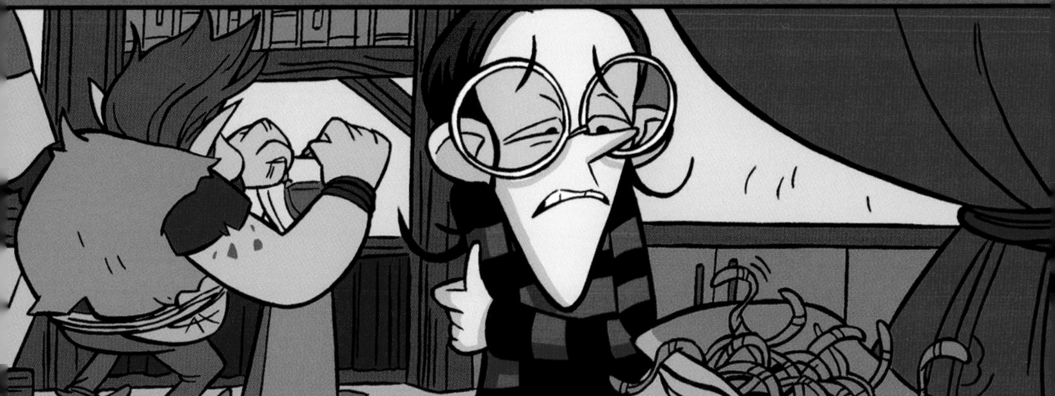

MAKE A PINE CONE TROLL

You can make your very own troll using some everyday objects and a pine cone!

What You Need:
- scissors
- felt
- glue
- two googly eyes
- a pine cone
- chenille stems
- two small corks
- decorations (such as shredded paper, leaves, grass, small pom-poms, buttons, or beads)

What You Do:
Step 1: To make the eyes, cut out small felt circles. Glue the googly eyes to the felt.

Step 2: Glue the felt eyes onto the pine cone.

Step 3: Twist two chenille stems together. Wrap the twisted stems around the middle of the pinecone. The ends should stick out to make arms.

Step 4: Cut out hand shapes from the felt. Glue them to the ends of the arm-stems.

Step 5: Glue two cork legs onto the bottom of the pine cone.

Step 6: Decorate your troll!

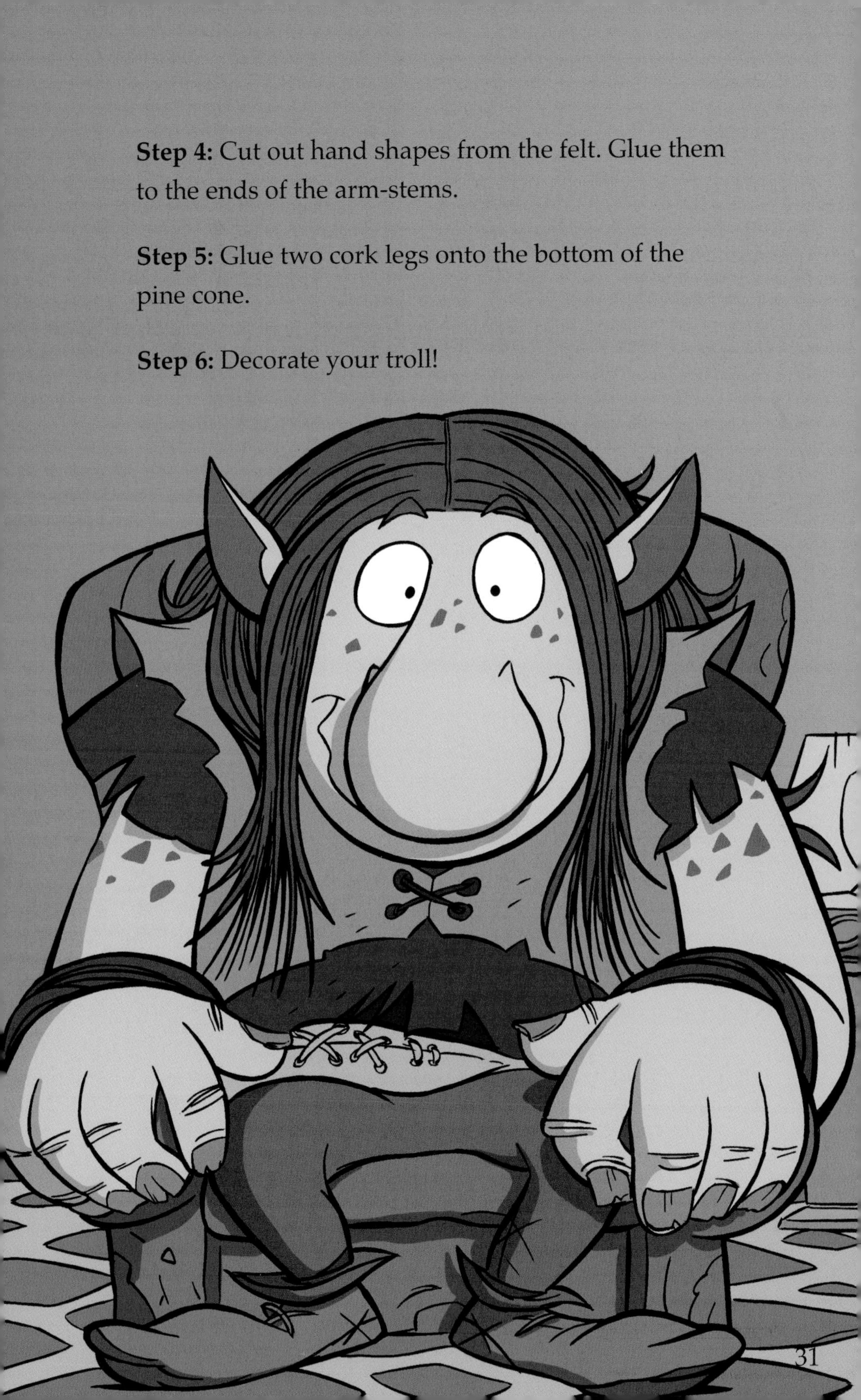

READ ALL THE AMAZING

DISCOVER GRAPHICS BOOKS!

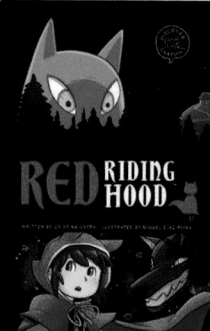